"Oh. Wow."

Jesse felt stunned...and humbled, as he registered the shape of their baby: the outline of the head and the body, even the skinny little legs and arms, and—most awesome and overwhelming—the rapid beating of the heart inside the chest.

He had some experience with ultrasounds—mostly with respect to equine fetuses. But this was completely outside his realm of experience. This was an actual human baby—his and Maggie's baby. He knew that he'd done very little to help grow this miracle inside her. Yes, he'd contributed half of the baby's DNA, but since then, he'd done nothing. She was the one who was giving their baby everything he or she needed, the only one who could.

He wanted to say something to express the awe and gratitude that filled his heart, but his throat was suddenly tight.

* * *

MONTANA MAVERICKS: 20 Years in the Saddle!

Dear Reader,

I can't believe it's been twenty years since the first Montana Mavericks book hit the shelves. In the past two decades, more than one hundred stories have been published under that banner, giving readers a glimpse of handsome and heroic cowboys from historical times to present day, from Whitehorn to Thunder Canyon to Rust Creek Falls and other places in between.

I am thrilled to be part of this twentieth anniversary celebration and especially to introduce you to small-town horse whisperer Jesse Crawford, who falls hard and fast for big-city corporate attorney Maggie Roarke. While it might appear that these two don't have much in common (aside from some serious chemistry!), discovering that their one night of passion is going to have long-term consequences might just be enough to bring this couple back together in time for a holiday happy-ever-after!

I hope you enjoy this return to Rust Creek Falls and *The Maverick's Thanksgiving Baby*.

Happy reading—and happy holidays!

Brenda Harlen

The Maverick's Thanksgiving Baby

—

Brenda Harlen

Special thanks and acknowledgment to Brenda Harlen for her contribution to the Montana Mavericks: 20 Years in the Saddle! continuity.

Recycling programs
for this product may
not exist in your area.

ISBN-13: 978-0-373-65848-0

The Maverick's Thanksgiving Baby

Printed in U.S.A.

HARLEQUIN®
www.Harlequin.com

Books by Brenda Harlen

BRENDA HARLEN

is a former family law attorney turned work-at-home mom and national bestselling author who has written more than twenty books for Harlequin. Her work has been validated by industry awards (including an RWA Golden Heart® Award and the *RT Book Reviews* Reviewers' Choice Award) and by the fact that her kids think it's cool that she's "a real author."

Brenda lives in southern Ontario with her husband and two sons. When she isn't at the computer working on her next book, she can probably be found at the arena, watching a hockey game. Keep up to date with Brenda on Facebook, follow her on Twitter, at @BrendaHarlen, or send her an email at brendaharlen@yahoo.com.

For Leanne Banks,

Who shared some honest truths about cowboys...
and other subjects :)

XO

Chapter One

July

Jesse Crawford was an idiot. A completely smitten and tongue-tied idiot.

But far worse than that indisputable fact was that Maggie Roarke now knew it, too.

What had ever possessed him to approach her? What had made him think he could introduce himself and have an actual conversation with a woman like her?

While he'd never been as smooth with women as any of his three brothers, he'd never been so embarrassingly inept, either. But being in close proximity to Maggie seemed to rattle his brain as completely as if he'd been thrown from the back of a horse—and that hadn't happened to him in more than fifteen years.

The first time he saw her, even before he knew her name, he'd been mesmerized. She was tall and willowy with subtle but distinctly feminine curves. Her blond hair spilled onto her shoulders like golden silk and her deep brown eyes could shine with humor or warm with compassion. And her smile—there was just something about her smile that seemed to reach right inside his chest and wrap around his heart. A ridiculously fanciful and foolish idea, of course, and one that he wouldn't dare acknowledge to anyone else.

It was no mystery to Jesse why a man would be attracted to her, but he was still a little mystified by the intensity of *his* reaction to her—especially when he didn't know the first thing about her. The discovery that she was a successful attorney in Los Angeles should have put an end to his ridiculous crush. Experience had proven to him that city girls didn't adapt well to the country, and there was no way a lawyer—from Hollywood of all places—would be interested in a small-town rancher. But still his long-guarded heart refused to be dissuaded.

He'd come to the official opening of the Grace Traub Community Center today because he knew she would be there, because he couldn't resist the opportunity to see her again, even from a distance. It had taken the better part of an hour for him to finally summon the courage to introduce himself. And when he did, without muttering or stumbling over words, he felt reassured that things weren't going too badly.

She offered her hand and, in that brief moment of contact, he'd been certain that he felt a real connection with her. And then she smiled at him, and all his carefully rehearsed words slid back down his throat, leaving him awe-struck and tongue-tied and destroying any hope he had of making a good first impression.

He'd almost been grateful that Arthur Swinton intruded on the moment, whisking her away for a private word. Jesse had stood there for another minute, watching her with the older man and wondering if she might come back to finish the conversation they hadn't even started. But Arthur had no sooner turned away when another man stepped into her path: Jared Winfree—also known as the Romeo of Rust Creek Falls.

The cowboy tipped his head down to talk to her. Maggie smiled at him, though Jesse noticed that her smile didn't seem to have the same debilitating effect on the other man, who leaned closer for a more intimate discussion. Jesse finally unglued his feet from the floor and walked out of the community center, berating himself for his awkwardness.

His cell phone started ringing before he'd hit the bottom step, and he pulled it out to answer the call. At this point, he didn't even care who was on the other end of the line—he was grateful for any distraction.

After a brief conversation with Brett Gable, he was feeling marginally better. The local rancher was having trouble with an ornery stallion and wondered if Jesse could take a look at him and let the owner know if he was wasting his time trying to tame the animal or if he just needed to adjust his tactics. Jesse promised that he'd go out to the Gable ranch the next day.

As he tucked his phone away again, he resolved to keep his focus on four-legged creatures and forget about women. Because while horses might not look as good or smell as pretty, they were a lot easier to understand and a lot less likely to trample all over his heart.

Or throw themselves into his arms?

"Whoa." Jesse caught her gently as she bounced off his chest.

Maggie's wide, startled gaze locked with his. "I'm so sorry," she said breathlessly.

"Everything okay?"

She shook her head, an introspective look now competing with the panic in her dark chocolate-colored eyes. "Are you married?"

"What?" He had no idea what thought process had precipitated the question, but he immediately shook his head. "No."

"Engaged? Involved?"

"No and no," he said, just a little warily.

"Then I'll apologize now and explain later," she told him.

"Apol—"

He'd intended to ask what she thought she needed to apologize for, but that was as far as he got before she lifted her hands to his shoulders and pressed her lips to his.

To say that he was stunned would have been an understatement. But the initial shock was quickly supplanted by other stronger emotions: pleasure, happiness, desire.

He wanted this. He wanted *her*. As if of their own volition, his arms wrapped around her, pulling her against him as he kissed her back.

Somewhere in a part of his brain that was still capable of registering anything beyond the heavenly feel of this woman in his arms, he heard the crunch of gravel beneath heavy, impatient footsteps and a frustrated voice muttering, "Where on earth could she have... Maggie?"

The woman in question eased her mouth from his.

There was desire in her eyes—he wasn't mistaken in that. But there was something else, too—a silent plea?

A plea for what, he didn't know and didn't care. Right now, he would have promised her anything. Everything.

She finally turned to look at the other man, and Jesse did the same.

Jared Winfree's brows were drawn together, his expression dark as he glanced from Maggie to Jesse. "Are you making a move on my woman?"

Since Jesse had no idea how to respond to that question, he was glad that Maggie spoke up.

"I'm not—and never have been—your woman," she told the Romeo.

But Jared continued to scowl. "We were supposed to be going to grab a bite to eat."

"No—you offered to take me for a bite to eat and I told you that I already had plans."

"With this guy?" His tone was skeptical.

She took Jesse's hand and lied without compunction. "We've been dating for the past several months."

"Then how come I've never seen you with him before?" Jared challenged.

"We've been trying to keep a low profile and avoid being the topic of gossip," she said easily.

It was obvious by the stormy look in the other guy's eyes that he wanted to challenge the claim, but with Maggie's hand linked with Jesse's and her lipstick on his mouth, the evidence was pretty convincing.

"When you decide you want a real cowboy, give me a call," Jared told her, and stormed off in the direction from which he'd come.

Maggie blew out a breath. "Thank goodness." She released the hand that she'd been holding on to as if it was a lifeline and turned to him. "And thank *you*."

"No need to thank me for something that was very much my pleasure," he assured her.

And the big-city lawyer with the razor-sharp mind and persuasive tongue actually blushed when his gaze dropped to linger on the sweet curve of her lips.

"Do you want me to explain now?" she asked.

"Only if you want to."

"I feel as if I owe you at least that much."

Half an hour earlier, he'd barely been able to say two words to her, but locking lips seemed to have loosened his, and he couldn't resist teasing her a little. "Or you could just kiss me again and we'll call it even."

Her mouth curved as she held his gaze, and he knew she was giving his offer serious consideration. "I think, for now, we'll go with the explanation."

"Your choice," he said.

"I met him at the Ace in the Hole a few months back,"

she began. "I was there to have lunch with my cousin, Lissa, but before we even had a chance to order, Lissa got called away. I decided to stay and at least finish my coffee, and he slid into the empty seat and introduced himself. He seemed friendly and we chatted for a while, but when he asked for my number, I told him I wasn't interested in starting anything up with someone in Rust Creek Falls because my life was in Los Angeles."

Which, Jesse reminded himself, was a fact he'd be wise to remember.

"He seemed to accept that easily enough and said maybe he'd see me around the next time I was in town. And I know Rust Creek Falls isn't a big city, but every single time I've been back since then, I've run into him. And every single time, he asks me to go out with him."

"So why didn't you just tell him you had a boyfriend in Los Angeles? I got the impression he would have believed that more readily than he believed you were with me."

"I don't think he would've believed anything without proof—which you're still wearing," she said, and lifted a hand to rub her lipstick off the corner of his mouth with her thumb.

And he felt it again—the sizzle and crackle of awareness when she touched him. And when her gaze locked on his, he knew that he wasn't the only one who had felt it.

"He hit on Lissa, too, when she first came to Rust Creek Falls," Maggie told him. "Apparently he even started a bar fight with some other guy who asked her to dance."

"I don't pay much attention to the gossip around town," Jesse said. "But I remember hearing about that—both the sheriff and his deputy got punched and two guys got arrested."

Maggie smiled. "Lissa insisted it wasn't her fault, but

Gage said something about beautiful women being the cause of most trouble at the Ace in the Hole."

"Then you better stay away from the bar or you might incite a riot."

Her cheeks colored prettily, as if she hadn't heard the same thing a thousand times before. And if she hadn't, he figured there was something seriously wrong with the guys in LA, because Maggie Roarke was a definite knockout.

"So why aren't you involved with anyone back home?" he asked now.

"How do you know I'm not?" she asked.

"You didn't kiss me until you'd confirmed that I wasn't seeing anyone, and I can't imagine you'd be any less respectful of your own relationship."

"You're right," she acknowledged. "As for not being involved—I guess I've just been too busy to do much dating."

"Until me," he teased.

She laughed. "Until you."

The magical sound of her soft laughter filled his heart, and the sparkle in her eyes took his breath away. He didn't know what else to say—or if he should say anything else at all. Maybe he should just walk away while she was smiling and hopefully not thinking that he was an idiot.

"I really do appreciate your cooperation," she told him. "If there's anything I can do to possibly repay the favor, I hope you'll ask."

"Well, I was planning to grab a burger at the Ace in the Hole," he admitted. "And despite the sheriff's warning to your cousin, I'd be willing to take the risk if you wanted to join me."

"Are you inviting me to have dinner with you?"

"It would substantiate your claim that we're dating."

"The Ace in the Hole?" she said dubiously.

He shrugged. "Since this isn't your first visit to Rust Creek Falls, you know that our options here are limited."

Still she hesitated, and Jesse began to suspect that her gratitude didn't actually extend to the point where she wanted to be seen in public with him. And that was okay. He understood what she'd been saying about small-town gossip, and he really didn't want to be put under the microscope any more than she did. But damn, he really did want to spend more time with her.

"I could do better than a burger," she finally said. "I could make dinner."

"You'd cook for me?"

"Which part surprises you the most—that I *can* cook or that I'm offering to cook for you?"

"I'm not sure," he admitted.

She laughed again. "At least you're honest."

"I guess I just thought, with you being a busy lawyer and all…"

"Lawyers have to eat on occasion, too," she said, when his explanation ran out.

"Yeah, but I would figure you've got a lot of dining options in LA."

"We do," she agreed. "But as it turns out, I like to cook. It helps me unwind at the end of the day. So what do you say—are you going to let me make you dinner?"

He was beginning to suspect that he would let Maggie Roarke do absolutely anything she wanted, but he figured dinner was a good start.

"An offer I can't refuse," he told her.

Maggie prided herself on the fact that she was an intelligent, educated woman. She'd graduated summa cum laude from Stanford Law School and was establishing a reputation for herself at Alliston & Blake—a prominent

Los Angeles law firm. She'd gone toe-to-toe with formidable opponents in the courtroom, she'd held her ground in front of arrogant judges and she'd refused to be impressed or intimidated by powerful clients. One of her greatest assets was her ability to remain calm and cool whatever the circumstances. She simply didn't get flustered.

But as Jesse followed her into Gage and Lissa's kitchen, she was definitely feeling flustered. There was just something about this shy, sexy cowboy that had her heart jumping around in her chest. She opened the refrigerator, peered inside.

"What do you like?" she asked.

He looked at her blankly.

"For dinner," she clarified.

He flashed a quick smile. "Sorry, I guess my mind wandered. As for food—I'm not fussy. I'll eat whatever you want to make."

"Chicken and pasta okay?" she asked him.

"Sure."

She took a package of chicken breasts out of the fridge, then rummaged for some other ingredients. She found green peppers in the crisper, onions in the pantry and a bowl of ripe tomatoes on the counter. But what she really needed was fresh basil, and Lissa didn't have any.

"Do you know if they carry fresh herbs at the General Store?"

"I doubt it," Jesse said. "You'd probably have to go into Kalispell for something like that."

"I can use dried," she admitted. "But fresh basil leaves would add a lot more visual appeal to the dish."

"I'm going to have dinner with a beautiful woman," he said. "That's enough visual appeal that I wouldn't mind if you made macaroni and cheese from a box."

She felt her cheeks heat. She'd received more effusive

compliments, but none had ever sounded as sincere. No one had looked at her the way he looked at her.

"Even without fresh basil, I do think this will be a step up from boxed mac and cheese."

She filled a pot with water and set it on the back burner, then drizzled some oil into a deep frying pan. While the oil heated, she sliced the chicken into strips and tossed them into the pan. As the chicken was cooking, she chopped up peppers and onions, then added those, too.

"Can I do anything to help?"

"You could open the wine," she suggested. "There's a bottle of Riesling in the fridge and glasses in the cupboard above."

He uncorked the bottle and poured the wine into two crystal goblets.

She dumped the pasta into the boiling water and set the timer, then took the glass he offered.

"To new friendships," he said, lifting his glass in a toast.

"To new friendships," she agreed. "And first dates."

"Is this a date?"

"Of course. Otherwise, I would have lied to Jared."

"We wouldn't want that," he teased.

She added the tomatoes to the frying pan, sprinkled in some of this and that, gave it a stir. Her movements were smooth and effortless, confirming her claim that she enjoyed cooking. Which was convenient, because he enjoyed eating.

Ten minutes later, he was sitting down to a steaming plate of penne pasta with chicken and peppers.

"This is really good," he told her.

"Better than mac and cheese from a box?"

"Much better."

They chatted while they ate, about anything and everything. She learned that he worked at his family's ranch, The

Shooting Star, but had his own house on the property, and that he was close to his siblings but was frequently baffled and frustrated by them. She confided that she sometimes felt smothered by her brothers, who tended to be a little overprotective, and admitted that she could have gone to work at Roarke & Associates—her parents' law firm—but wanted to establish her own reputation in the field.

She had a second glass of wine while he had a second serving of pasta, and they lingered at the table. He was easy to talk to, and he actually listened to what she was saying. As a result, she found herself telling him things she'd never told anyone else, such as her concern that she'd been so focused on her career that she hadn't given much thought to anything else, and she was starting to wonder if she'd ever find the time to get married and have a family.

Not that she was in any hurry to do so, she hastened to explain. After all, she was only twenty-eight years old. But she was admittedly worried that if she continued on the same course, she might be so focused on her billable hours that she wouldn't even hear her biological clock when it started ticking.

Jesse told her that he'd gone to Montana State University to study Animal Science, graduating with a four-year degree. As for dating, he confided that he hadn't done much of that, either, claiming that most of the women in town had gone out with one or more of his brothers and he had no intention of trying to live up to their reputations.

After the meal was finished, he insisted on helping with the cleanup. While she put the dishes into the dishwasher, he washed the pans.

She'd enjoyed spending time with Jesse, and she wasn't eager for the night to end. He was smart and interesting and definitely easy to look at, and despite the underlying hum of attraction, she felt comfortable with him—or at least she did until he turned to reach for a towel at the same moment that she straightened up to close the door of the dishwasher and the back of his hand inadvertently brushed the side of her breast.

She sucked in a breath; he snatched his hand back.

"I'm so sorry."

"No, it was my fault."

But fault was irrelevant. What mattered was that the air was fairly crackling and sizzling with awareness now. And the way he looked at her—his gaze heated and focused— she was certain he felt it, too.

She barely knew him. But she knew she'd never felt the same immediacy and intensity of connection that she felt the minute he'd taken her hand inside the community center only a few hours earlier. But she was a Los Angeles attorney and he was a Rust Creek cowboy, and she knew that chemistry—as compelling as it might be—could not bridge the gap between them.

And Jesse had obviously come to the same conclusion, because he took a deliberate step back, breaking the threads of the seductive web that had spun around them. "I should probably be on my way."

"Oh." She forced a smile and tried to ignore the sense of disappointment that spread through her. "Okay."

She followed him to the door.

He paused against the open portal. "Thanks again for dinner."

"You're welcome," she said. "And if you ever need a fictional girlfriend to get you out of a tight spot, feel free to give me a call."

He lifted a hand and touched her cheek, the stroke of his fingertips over her skin making her shiver. "I don't want a fictional girlfriend, but I do want to kiss you for real."

She wasn't sure if he was stating a fact or asking permission, but before she could respond, he'd lowered his head and covered her mouth with his.

She might have caught him off guard when she'd pressed her lips to his outside of the community center, but it hadn't taken him long to respond, to take control of the kiss. This time, he was in control right from the beginning—she didn't have a chance to think about what he was doing or brace herself against the wave of emotions that washed over her.

For a man who claimed he didn't do a lot of dating, he sure knew how to kiss. His mouth was warm and firm as it moved over hers, masterfully persuasive and seductive. Never before had she been kissed with such patient thoroughness. His hands were big and strong, but infinitely gentle as they slid up her back, burning her skin through the silky fabric of her blouse as he urged her closer. Her breasts were crushed against the solid wall of his chest, and her nipples immediately responded to the contact, tightening into rigid peaks.

She wanted him to touch her—she wanted those callused hands on her bare skin, and the fierceness of the want was shocking. Equally strong was the desire to touch him—to let her hands roam over his rock-hard body, exploring and savoring every inch of him. He was so completely and undeniably male, and he made everything that was female inside of her quiver with excitement.

Eventually, reluctantly, he eased his mouth from hers. But he kept his arms around her, as if he couldn't bear to let her go. "I should probably be on my way before the sheriff gets home."

"He won't be home tonight," she admitted. "He and Lissa went to Bozeman for the weekend."

He frowned at that. "You're going to be alone here tonight?"

She held his gaze steadily. "I hope not."

He closed the door and turned the lock.

Chapter Two

November

Jesse had tossed the last bag of broodmare supplement into the back of his truck when he saw a pair of shiny, high-heeled boots stop beside the vehicle. He wiped the back of his hand over his brow and lifted his head to find Lissa Christensen, Maggie's cousin and also the sheriff's wife, standing there.

He touched a hand to the brim of his hat. "Mrs. Christensen," he said politely.

"It's Lissa," she told him, and offered a smile that was both warm and apologetic.

He wondered what she felt she had to apologize for. Maggie had told him that Lissa wasn't just her cousin— she was her best friend—and he would bet that whatever Maggie's reasons for ending their relationship before it had really even begun, she would have confided in the other woman. No doubt Lissa knew more than he wanted her to, but she didn't need to know—he wouldn't let her see—how hurt he'd been by Maggie's decision.

"Is there something I can help you with, ma'am?"

"Actually, I'm here to help you."

"While I appreciate the offer, I'm already finished," he said, deliberately misunderstanding her.

She shook her head, clearly exasperated with him. "Have you talked to Maggie recently?"

"Can't say that I have," he said, his tone carefully neutral.

"You need to talk to her," Lissa insisted. "Sooner rather than later."

And though Jesse's heart urged him to reach out to her once again, Maggie had trampled on it once already and he wasn't eager to give her another chance. Maybe pride was cold comfort without the warmth of the woman in his arms, but it was all he had left, and that pride wouldn't let him continue to chase after a woman who had made it clear she wasn't interested.

"If your cousin wants to talk, she knows where to find me," he countered.

Lissa huffed out a breath. "If nothing else, the two of you have obstinacy in common."

He closed the tailgate of his truck. "If that's all you wanted to say, I need to get back to Traub Stables."

"There's plenty more to say," she told him. "But it's not for me to say it."

He lifted his brows in response to that cryptic comment as he moved to the driver's-side door.

"Please talk to her," Lissa urged again.

He slid behind the wheel and drove away, but her insistence nagged at the back of his mind all the way back to Traub Stables. Lissa had to know that he'd been out of touch with her cousin for a while, so why was she all fired up about him needing to talk to Maggie? Why now?

Oddly enough, he'd got a phone call—out of the blue—just a few days earlier from his former fiancée. Shaelyn had said she wanted to talk, so he'd told her to talk. Then she'd said she wanted to see him, but he hadn't thought there was any point in that. Now he was wondering why the women from his past, who had already tossed him aside, had suddenly decided he was worthy of their attention.

He continued to puzzle over his recent conversation with Lissa as he worked with a spirited yearling. And because he was thinking about her cousin, when he got the feeling that someone was watching him, he instinctively knew that someone was Maggie.

He hadn't seen her since July, and the passing of time was evidenced by the changing of the season. When he'd met her the day of the community center opening, she'd been wearing a slim-fitting skirt and high-heeled sandals that showed her long, slender legs to full advantage along with a sleeveless silky blouse that highlighted her feminine curves. Today she was bundled up in a long winter coat that he'd bet she'd borrowed from her cousin since she wouldn't have much use for one in Los Angeles. In addition to the coat, she was wearing a red knitted hat with a pom-pom and matching red mittens, and even from a distance, he could see that her cheeks were pink from the cold.

Her choice to stand outside, he decided. And though it was obvious to both of them that she was waiting for him, he refused to cut the yearling's workout short. He wasn't being paid to slack off, and he wasn't going to let her distract him from his job. Even when she hadn't been there, she'd been too much of a distraction over the past several months.

While he continued to work with the filly, he cautioned himself against speculating on the purpose of her visit. He didn't know why she was there or how long she planned to stay this time, but he knew it would be foolish to expect anything from her. He finished running the young horse through her exercises before he passed her off to one of the stable hands for cooldown and grooming and finally turned his attention to Maggie.

"Hello, Jesse."

She looked good. Better than good. She looked like everything he'd ever wanted in a woman, and he knew that she was. He also knew that she was definitely out of his reach.

He nodded in acknowledgment of her greeting. "When did you get back into town?" he asked, his tone polite but cool.

"Last night."

Which confirmed that she'd already been in Rust Creek Falls when he ran into her cousin at the feed store— suggesting that Lissa's appearance there had not been a coincidence. "More of Arthur Swinton's business?"

She shook her head. "I came to see you."

And damn if his heart didn't kick against his ribs like an ornery stallion trying to break out of its stall. Because he was feeling more than he wanted to feel, more than he intended to admit, the single word was harsh when he asked, "Why?"

"I need to talk to you."

"Isn't that what we're doing now?"

"Please, Jesse. Can we go somewhere a little more private?"

He wanted to refuse. He definitely didn't want to be alone with her, because that would undoubtedly remind him of the last time he'd been alone with her—the night they'd made love.

"I wouldn't be asking if it wasn't important," she said.

"Do you know where The Shooting Star is?" he asked, naming his family's ranch.

She nodded.

"My house is the first one on the left, after the driveway splits. Can you meet me there in an hour?"

She nodded without hesitation. "That would be good."

No, good would've been if she'd come back three months sooner and asked to be alone with him. Then he would have been sure that they both wanted the same thing. Now, after so much time had passed, he had no idea what she wanted, what she thought they needed to talk about.

But he knew she'd been gone 119 days, and wasn't that pathetic? He'd actually been counting the days. At first, he'd been counting in anticipation of her return. More recently, he'd been counting in the hope that with each day that passed he would be one day closer to forgetting about her.

And he'd been certain he was getting there—but only five minutes in her company had him all churned up inside again, wanting what he knew he couldn't have.

What was she going to do for an hour?

She slid behind the wheel of her rental car and considered her options. She was less than five minutes away from Gage and Lissa's house, but she didn't want to go back there. Her cousin hadn't stopped nagging her since she'd got into town the night before. Not that Lissa had said anything Maggie hadn't already thought herself.

She pulled out of the parking lot and back onto the road, heading toward town. She drove down Falls Street, turned onto Sawmill, crossing over the bridge without any destination in mind. She was only killing time, watching the minutes tick away until the allotted hour had passed.

Her phone buzzed to indicate receipt of a text message, so she turned onto Main and pulled into an empty park-

ing spot by Crawford's General Store to dig her phone out
of her purse.

Have you seen him yet?

    The message, not surprisingly, was from Lissa.
    Mtg him at SS @ 4, she texted back.
    Good luck! her cousin replied.
    Maggie was afraid she was going to need it.
    Since she had her phone in hand, she decided to check
her email from work. There wasn't anything urgent, but re-
sponding to the messages helped her kill some more time.
    She knew that she was stalling, thinking about anything
but the imminent conversation with Jesse. Now that there
were less than twenty minutes before their scheduled meeting, she should be focused on that, thinking about what
she was going to say, how to share her news.
    She'd hoped to take her cue from him—but the few
words that they'd exchanged at Traub Stables hadn't given
her a hint about what he was thinking. His gaze had been
shuttered, but the coolness of his tone had been a strong
indication that he was finished with her. It wasn't even that
he was over her—it was as if they'd never been.
    Maybe she shouldn't have come back. Maybe this was
a monumental mistake. It was obvious that he felt nothing for her—maybe he never had. Maybe the magic of that
night had only ever existed in her imagination.
    But she didn't really believe that. She certainly hadn't
imagined the numerous phone calls, text messages and
emails they'd exchanged every single day for the first couple of weeks. And during those early weeks, he'd seemed
eager for her to come back to Rust Creek Falls, as anxious
to be with her again as she was to be with him.
    She'd originally planned to return in the middle of Au-

gust, but only two days before her scheduled trip one of the senior partners had asked for her help with an emergency injunction for an important client threatened by a hostile takeover. Of course, that injunction had only been the first step in a long process of corporate restructuring, and Maggie had been tapped for assistance every step of the way.

She'd enjoyed the challenge and the work and knew it had been good for her career. Unfortunately, it had consumed almost every waking minute and had signaled the beginning of the end of her relationship with Jesse. Four months was a long time to be apart, and he'd obviously moved on.

She rubbed a hand over her chest, where her heart was beating dully against her breastbone. The possibility that their passionate lovemaking could have been so readily forgotten cut her to the quick. Maybe it was irrational and unreasonable, but she'd started to fall in love with him that night. Even when she'd said goodbye to him the next day, she didn't think it was the end of their relationship but only the beginning.

Of course, her emotions were her responsibility. He'd never made her any promises; he'd certainly never said that he was in love with her. But the way he'd kissed her and touched her and loved her—with his body if not his heart—she'd been certain there was something special between them, something more than a one-night affair. She didn't think she'd imagined that, but even if the connection had been real, it was obviously gone now, and the pain of that loss made her eyes fill with tears.

Blinking them away, she pulled from the curb and headed toward The Shooting Star.

Jesse's house was a beautiful if modest two-story with white siding, a wide front porch and lots of windows flanked by deep green shutters.

His truck in the driveway confirmed that he was home, and he opened the door before she even had a chance to knock.

"You're punctual," he said, stepping back so that she could enter.

"I appreciate you making the time to see me."

He shrugged. "You said it was important."

"It is," she confirmed.

She continued to stand just inside the door, looking at him, wanting to memorize all the little details she was afraid she might have forgotten over the past four months.

The breadth of his shoulders beneath the flannel shirt he wore, the rippling strength of his abdominal muscles, the strength of those wide-palmed hands. The way his mouth curved just a little higher on the left side when he smiled; the almost-imperceptible scar on his chin, the result of a misstep as he'd climbed over a fence when he was eight years old. His hair was damp, as if he'd recently stepped out of the shower, and his jaw was freshly shaven, tempting her to reach up and touch the smooth skin.

"Do you want to take your coat off?"

"Sure." But she pulled off her mittens and hat first, tucking them into the pockets of the long coat she'd borrowed from her cousin. When she finally stripped off the heavy garment, he took it from her, hanging it on a hook by the door, beside his Sherpa-lined leather jacket.

"Keep your boots on," he said when she reached down to untie them. "The floor's probably cold."

It might have been true, but the abruptness of his tone suggested that he didn't want her to get too comfortable or stay for too long. She kept her boots on, but wiped them carefully on the mat before stepping off it.

The main floor plan was open, with a dining area on one side and a living room on the other. The furniture was distressed leather with nail-head trim, oversize and masculine in design but perfect for the open space. Flames were crackling inside the river-rock fireplace, providing the room with both warmth and ambience. Jesse had moved to the kitchen, separated from the dining room by a long, granite-topped counter.

"Do you want a cup of tea?" he asked, already filling the kettle.

"That would be nice, thank you."

Even she winced at the cool politeness of their conversation. It was as if they were strangers meeting for the first time rather than lovers who had spent hours naked together. Yes, it had only been one night, but it had been the most incredible night of her life. The way he'd touched her, with his hands and his lips and his body, had introduced her to heights of pleasure she'd never imagined.

Even now, the memories of that night made her cheeks flush and her heart pound. Though it took a determined effort, she pushed them aside and forced herself to focus on the here and now.

"You've lost weight," he noted, his gaze skimming over her.

"A few pounds," she admitted. Actually, she'd been down nine pounds a couple of months earlier, but she'd managed to gain six of them back.

Jesse studied her carefully, noting the bony outline of her shoulders in the oversize sweater she wore over slim-fitting jeans, and guessed that she'd lost more than a few pounds. She was pale, too, and those beautiful brown eyes that had haunted his dreams looked even bigger and darker than he remembered.

The last time they'd spoken on the phone, she'd told him that she'd been feeling unwell, fighting some kind of virus. He'd thought it was just the latest in a long line of excuses for why she'd chosen not to return to Rust Creek Falls. It seemed apparent now that there had been at least some truth in her explanation.

He poured the boiling water into a mug, over a bag of peppermint tea. The day that she'd made him dinner, she'd told him it was her favorite flavor. And, sap that he was, he'd not only remembered but had bought a box so that he'd have it on hand when she came to visit.

The box had sat, unopened, in his cupboard for almost four months. Now, finally, she was going to have a cup—and the other eleven bags would probably sit in the box in his cupboard for another four months before he finally tossed them in the trash.

"Are you feeling okay?" he asked.

She looked up, as if startled by the question.

"You said that you'd been fighting some kind of virus," he reminded her. "I just wondered if you've fully recovered from whatever it was you had."

She wrapped her hands around the warm mug. "I'm feeling much better, thanks."

"It must have been quite a bug, to have laid you up for so long," he commented.

"It wasn't a bug." She lifted her gaze to his. "It was—*is*—a baby."

Jesse stared at her for a long minute, certain he couldn't have heard her correctly.

"A baby?" he finally echoed.

She nodded. "I'm pregnant."

He hated to ask, but he hadn't seen her since July and he knew he'd be a fool if he didn't. "Is it…mine?"

He held his breath, waiting for her response, not sure if he wanted it to be yes or no. Not sure how he would feel either way.

She winced at the question. "Yes, it's yours."

"I'm sorry," he said automatically.

"That it's yours?"

"That I had to ask," he clarified.

But she shook her head. "I knew you would. If you were one of my clients, I'd insist that you get proof," she admitted. "And if you want a DNA test, I'll give it to you, but there isn't any other possibility. I haven't been with anyone else in more than two years."

"You're pregnant with my child," he said, as if repeating the words might somehow help them to make sense.

His thoughts were as jumbled as his emotions. Joy warred with panic inside of him as he realized that he was going to be a father—a prospect that was as terrifying as it was exciting.

"I'm not here because I want or expect anything from you," she explained. "I just thought you should know about the baby."

Irritation bubbled to the surface. "I don't know which part of that outrageous statement to deal with first."

"Excuse me?"

"We made that baby together," he reminded her. "So you should want and expect plenty.

"As for letting me know—should I thank you for finally, in the fourth month of pregnancy, telling me that you're going to have my child?"

She winced at the harsh accusation in his tone. "It's not as if I was deliberately keeping my pregnancy a secret."

"You were accidentally keeping it a secret?"

"I didn't know."

He stared at her in disbelief. "You didn't know?"

"I didn't," she insisted.

"I'm sure you didn't figure it out yesterday."

"No," she admitted. "But for the first few weeks after I returned to LA, I was so busy with work that I thought the

fatigue and nausea were symptoms of my erratic sched-
ule and not sleeping well or eating properly. Even when
I missed my first period—" her cheeks flushed, as if she
was uncomfortable talking about her monthly cycle despite
the intimacies they'd shared "—I didn't think anything of
it. I've skipped periods before, usually when I'm stressed."

He scowled but couldn't dispute her claim. Instead he
asked, "So when did you first suspect you might be pregnant?"

"Mid-September. And even then, it was my mother who
brought up the possibility. Which I didn't think was a possibility, because we were careful both times."

Both times. He didn't carry condoms in his wallet anymore, and she'd only had two in her makeup case. So they'd
done all kinds of things to pleasure one another but they'd
only made love twice.

And both times had felt like heaven on earth—the
merging of their bodies had been so perfect, so right—

He severed the unwelcome memory.

"So I took a home pregnancy test." She continued her
explanation. "And even when it showed a positive result,
I wasn't sure I believed it. The next day, my doctor confirmed the result."

"This was mid-September?" he prompted.

She nodded again.

"So you've known for six weeks, and you only decided
to tell me now?"

"I didn't know how to tell you," she admitted. "It wasn't
the kind of news I wanted to share over the phone, and my
doctor advised me not to travel until the morning sickness
was under control."

"Did you ever think to invite me to come out to LA to
see you?"

She blinked, confirming his suspicion that she had not.

That the possibility of reaching out to him had not once entered her mind. "You never showed any interest in making a trip to California."

"If you'd asked, if you'd said that you needed to see me, I would have come." And he would have been glad to do so, overjoyed by the prospect of seeing her again.

"I'm sorry," she said. "I never thought… And when I called to tell you that my planned visit to Rust Creek Falls was further delayed, you sounded as if you'd already written me off. And that's okay," she hastened to assure him. "I know neither of us expected that one night together would have such long-lasting repercussions."

"I didn't think it was going to be only one night," he told her.

"I bet you didn't think you'd end up having this conversation four months later, either," she said.

"No," he agreed.

"I know you've only had a few minutes to think about this, but I wanted you to know that I'm planning to keep the baby."

He scowled, because it hadn't occurred to him that she might want to do anything else. "You thought about giving away our baby?"

"There were a few moments—especially in the beginning—when I wasn't sure what I would do," she admitted. "I was stunned and scared—having a baby at this stage of my life wasn't anywhere in my plans."

"You don't just give away a baby because it wasn't in your plans," he told her.

"Some people do," she told him.

Only then did he remember that she was adopted, given up by her sixteen-year-old birth mother when she was only a few days old.

While he was busy trying to extract his foot from his

mouth, she continued, "And not necessarily because it's the easy choice. I don't know whether my birth mother wanted to keep me or not—Christa and Gavin always told me that she recognized that she couldn't give me the kind of life that I had with my parents, and I've always been grateful to her for that. So yes, I thought about giving up my baby, because I know that's sometimes the best option.

"But," she continued before he could protest, "I don't think it is for my baby. And maybe it's maternal instinct or maybe it's because I was adopted, but I felt an immediate bond with this baby who shares my DNA, and I can't even imagine letting him or her go."

"The baby shares half of your DNA," he pointed out. "The other half is mine."

She nodded. "And if you want to be part of our baby's life, I'd be happy to accommodate whatever kind of visitation you—"

"Visitation?" he interrupted, his voice dangerously soft.

She eyed him warily. "If that's what you want."

"It's not."

"Oh. Okay. In that case, I'll have papers drawn up—"

He interrupted her again. "The only paper we're going to need is a marriage license."

Chapter Three

Maggie stared at him, certain she couldn't have heard him correctly. "Excuse me?"

"We're having a baby together, which means we should get married to raise that child together." His tone was implacable.

"You can't be serious."

"Of course I'm serious. I'm not going to shirk my responsibilities."

"There's a lot of ground between shirking responsibility and marriage," she said, determined to remain calm and reasonable despite the outrageousness of his proposition.

"I want to be a father to my child."

"You are the baby's father."

"I want the baby to have my name."

She'd been so apprehensive about this meeting—worried about how he'd respond to the news of her pregnancy. Obviously she knew he'd be surprised, and she'd prepared herself for the possibility that he might deny paternity. But in all of the scenarios that she'd envisioned, she'd never once considered that he might propose marriage. And while she'd feared that he might reject both her and the baby, his grim determination to do "the right thing" was somehow worse.

This wasn't at all how she'd planned things to happen in her life. Yes, she wanted to get married someday. Her parents had given all of their children the wonderful example of a true partnership, and Maggie wanted to find the same forever kind of love someday. And when she did, she would get married and *then* have a baby. So while she hadn't planned to get pregnant just yet, she didn't intend to change anything aside from the order of things. She would be the best mother she could be to her child, but she wasn't going to settle for a loveless marriage with a stubborn cowboy—even if his kisses had the power to make her lose all sense and reason.

If Jesse had been offering her something more... If he'd given any indication that he'd been genuinely happy to see her, if he'd wrapped his arms around her and kissed her with even half of the passion and enthusiasm she knew he was capable of, she might have ignored all of her questions and doubts and followed him to the nearest wedding chapel. But the coolness of his initial response to her return to Rust Creek Falls proved that he didn't want her—he only wanted to ensure the legitimacy of his child.

"We don't have to get married for your name to go on the baby's birth certificate," she told him. "I would never deny my child's paternity."

"*Our* child," he reminded her. "And it's about more than just a name. It's about giving our baby the family he or she deserves."

"What about what *we* deserve?" she challenged. "Don't you want to fall in love and exchange vows with someone you really want to be with instead of someone you inadvertently got pregnant?"

"What I want—what you want—isn't as important as what our baby needs," he insisted stubbornly.

She blew out a breath. "I don't think our baby needs to be raised by two parents trapped in a loveless marriage."

"You don't have to make it sound so dire. If we want to, we can make this work."

"What if I don't want to?"

He ignored her question as if she hadn't even spoken. "We should be able to make all of the necessary arrangements for a wedding within a couple of weeks."

"Did you get kicked in the head by a horse? I am *not* marrying you."

The lift of his brows was the only indication that he'd heard her this time, as he steamrollered over her protest. "We can have a quick courthouse ceremony here or a more traditional wedding in LA, if you prefer."

"So I *do* have some say in this?"

"The details," he agreed. "I don't care about the where and when so long as it's legal."

There was something about his determination to make her his wife that thrilled her even as it infuriated her. And she suspected that, deep in her heart, she wanted what he was offering: to get married and raise their baby together.

But she didn't want a marriage on the terms he was offering. She didn't want a legal union for the sake of their baby but a commitment based on mutual respect and affection. Unfortunately, that offer wasn't on the table. And even if it was, there were other obstacles to consider.

"What about the detail also known as my job?" she challenged.

"What about it?"

"How am I going to represent my clients in Los Angeles if I'm living in Rust Creek Falls? Or am I supposed to happily sacrifice all of my career ambitions for the pleasure of becoming Mrs. Jesse Crawford?"

His only response was a scowl that proved he hadn't given much thought to the distance that separated them geographically.

"I'm sure you can find a job in Rust Creek Falls, if you want to keep working."

"Or maybe you could find work in Los Angeles," she countered.

"Now you're just being ridiculous."

"And you're being completely unreasonable."

"It's not unreasonable to want our child to be raised by two parents."

"Look at us, Jesse. We can't even have a simple conversation without fighting and you want us to get married?"

"Yes, I do," he said again.

She shook her head. "Obviously we have a fundamental difference of opinion."

"I don't recall there being any differences of opinion when we were in bed together."

And with those words, the air was suddenly charged with electricity.

The heat in his gaze spread warmth through her veins, from her belly to her breasts, throbbing between her thighs. He wasn't even touching her—and she was fairly quivering with desire.

No one had ever affected her the way this man did. No one had ever made her feel the way she felt when she was with him. But even more unnerving than the wanting of her body was the yearning of her heart.

She pushed away from the breakfast bar and carried her empty mug to the sink. She had to leave, to give them both some time and space to think about how they should proceed.

"Maggie."

She looked up, and he was there. Close enough that she couldn't breathe without inhaling his clean, masculine scent. Close enough that he had to hear her heart pounding. And although his eyes never left hers, she felt the heat of his gaze everywhere.

He lifted a hand to touch her hair, his fingers skimming over the silky tresses to cradle the back of her head. Then his mouth was on hers, his lips warm and firm and sure, and she melted against him.

She'd forgotten how strong he was, how solid every inch of his body was. Hard and unyielding. And yet, for all of his strength, he was incredibly gentle. It was that unadulterated masculine strength combined with his inherently gentle nature that had appealed to her from the first.

His hands slid down her back, inched up beneath the hem of her sweater. Then those wide, callused palms were on her skin, sliding up her torso to cup her breasts. Her blood pulsed in her veins, hot and demanding. His thumbs brushed over her nipples through the delicate lace, and she actually whimpered.

He nibbled on her lips. Teasing, tasting, tempting.

"I want you, Maggie."

She wanted him, too. And though she knew it might be a mistake to let herself succumb to that desire while there was still so much unresolved between them, that knowledge didn't dampen her need.

"Tell me you feel the same," he urged.

"I do," she admitted. "But—"

She forgot the rest of what she'd intended to say when he lifted her off her feet and into his arms.

He carried her up the stairs and down a short hallway to his bedroom with effortless ease. When he set her on her feet beside the bed, she knew that if she was going to protest, now was the time to do so. Then he kissed her again, and any thought of protest flew out of her mind.

Her mouth parted beneath the pressure of his, and his tongue swept inside, teasing the soft inside of her lips. His hands slid down her back, over the curve of her buttocks, pulling her close. The evidence of his arousal fueled her own. Blood pulsed in her veins, pooled low in her belly, making her want so much that she actually ached.

She lifted her hands to the buttons of his shirt and began

to unfasten them. She wanted to touch him, to feel the warmth of his bare skin beneath her palms. But the cotton T-shirt under the flannel impeded her efforts. With a frustrated sigh, she tugged the T-shirt out of his jeans and shoved her hands beneath it.

Jesse chuckled softly. "I didn't realize this was a race."

"I want to feel your body against mine," she confessed.

He released her long enough to get rid of his clothes. She sat on the edge of the bed, intending to do the same, but she was still struggling with her boots when his jeans hit the floor. As he kicked them away, she couldn't help but admire the knit boxer briefs that molded to the firm muscles of his buttocks and thighs at the back and did absolutely nothing to hide the obvious evidence of his arousal at the front.

Her mouth went dry and her fingers froze on the knotted laces. He knelt beside her and efficiently untied the boots and pulled them from her feet. Then he unfastened her jeans and pushed them over her hips, down her legs, finally stripping them away along with her socks.

"Your feet are cold," he realized, warming them between his palms. "You need thicker socks."

Not in California, she thought, but didn't say it aloud. She didn't want to speak of the distance that separated their lives; she didn't want anything to take away from the here and now.

"Or I could get under the covers," she suggested.

"That's a better plan," he agreed.

But first, he lifted her sweater over her head and tossed it aside, leaving her clad in only a lace demi-cup bra and matching bikini panties. He sat back on his haunches, the heat in his gaze roaming over her as tangible as a caress, making her nipples tighten and her thighs quiver.

"You absolutely take my breath away," he told her.

She tugged the covers down and rolled over the bed to

snuggle beneath them. Jesse immediately slid in beside her, his hands skimming over her, tracing her curves. He lowered his head to nuzzle the tender skin at the base of her throat, making her shiver.

He glanced up. "Are you still cold?"

She shook her head; he smiled slightly before he lowered his head again, his lips skimming across her collarbone, then tracing the lacy edge of her bra. She could feel his breath, warm on her skin, as his mouth hovered above her breast. Her hand lifted to his head, silently urging him closer. He willingly acquiesced to her direction, laving her nipple with his tongue. The sensation of hot, wet heat through the silky fabric made her gasp, then his lips closed over the lace-covered peak, sending fiery spears of pleasure arrowing to her core.

He found the center clasp of her bra and released it, peeling the fabric aside so he could suckle her bare flesh, making her groan. He tugged the straps down her arms, dropped the garment to the floor. His hands stroked down her torso, his fingers hooking in her panties and dragging them down her legs and away, so that she was completely naked. All the while, his hands and his lips moved over her, teasing and tempting, until her body was fairly quivering with wanting.

Genetics had blessed her with a naturally slim build and the loss of those few pounds had pushed her from slender toward skinny, but she knew that was only a temporary state. Because although her hip bones and ribs were visible now, there was also a subtle roundness to her belly—evidence of the baby she carried.

He splayed his hand over the curve, his wide palm covering her almost from hip bone to hip bone, as if cradling their child, and the sweetness of the gesture made tears fill her eyes.

"Everyone says that a baby is a miracle," he said. "But

the idea of you growing our baby inside of you is every bit as miraculous."

"You call it *miraculous* now. In a few more months, you'll be calling it *fat*."

She'd been teasing, attempting to lighten the mood, but as soon as she spoke the words, she wished she could take them back. Talking about the future as if they would be together was a mistake, even if it was—deep in her heart—what she wanted.

But he shook his head. "You'll always be beautiful to me—the most beautiful woman I've ever known."

Which might have sounded like a well-rehearsed line from another man, but the sincerity in his tone made her heart swell inside her chest.

"I want to be with you through every step of your pregnancy," he continued. "I want to see the changes in your body as our baby grows. I want to be the one who runs to the grocery store in the middle of the night when you have a sudden craving for ice cream."

"I didn't think the store in Rust Creek Falls was open in the middle of the night."

"Lucky for you, I have a key."

"That is lucky," she agreed. "But I don't want to worry about the future right now."

"What do you want?"

She lifted her arms to link them behind his neck. "You. I only want you."

"Well, that's convenient," he said. "Because I want you, too."

Then he captured her mouth in a long, slow kiss that went on and on until her head was actually spinning. The hand that was on her belly inched lower. His fingers sifted through the soft curls at the apex of her thighs and her hips automatically lifted off the bed, wordlessly encouraging his exploration. He parted the slick folds and dipped inside. She didn't know if it was the pregnancy hormones or Jesse, but all it took was that one stroke, deep inside, and she flew apart.

He continued to stroke her while the convulsions rippled through her body. Her hands fisted in the sheet, as she tried to anchor herself against the onslaught of sensations. "Jesse, please."

He leaned forward to reach into the drawer beside his bed and pulled out a small square packet.

Though she was reassured by this evidence of what was obviously a long-ingrained habit, she had to smile. "Isn't that a little like closing the barn door after the horse is out?"

"I guess it is," he agreed. "Although there are more reasons than pregnancy for using protection."

"Oh." She blushed. "Of course."

"But there's been no one since you," he said sincerely. "And no one for more than six months before that."

She took the square packet out of his hand. "Then we don't need this," she said, and set it on the bedside table.

He parted her legs and settled between them, burying himself deep in one thrust as she arched up to meet him.

He groaned in appreciation as she wrapped her legs around his hips. "You feel…so…good."

"You make me feel good," she told him.

He smiled at that and lowered his head to kiss her, long and slow and deep, as he moved inside her.

Maggie had never thought of herself as a particularly sensual woman. She certainly wasn't the type to get carried away by passion. She'd always thought sex was enjoyable, if unremarkable, but that was before she'd had sex with Jesse.

Over the past few months, she'd decided that her memories of the one night they'd spent together had been exaggerated by her imagination. It wasn't really possible that just standing close to him had made her knees weak, that breathing in his unique scent could make her insides quiver, that the touch of his mouth against her was enough to make her bones melt. Of course it wasn't. For some reason, she'd romanticized the memory, turned their one-night affair into something it never was and was never meant to be.

And then she'd seen him again, and her knees had gone weak. He'd stepped closer to her, and her insides had quivered. It didn't matter that his gaze had been guarded and his tone had been cool. All that mattered was he was there, and every nerve ending in her body was suddenly and acutely aware of him, aching for him.

Then, finally, he'd touched her. Just a brush of his hand over her hair, but that was enough to have her heart hammering inside of her chest. And then he kissed her, and not just her bones but everything inside of her had melted into a puddle of need. There was no thought or reason, there was only want. Hot and sharp and desperate.

As he moved inside of her now, she felt the connection between them. Not just the physical mating of their bodies but the joining of their souls. Maybe it was fantastical, but it was how she felt. She couldn't think of anything but Jesse, didn't want anyone but him.

The delicious friction between their bodies was every bit as incredible as she'd remembered—maybe even more. Every stroke, every thrust, sent little shock waves zinging through her blood. She could feel the anticipation building inside of her. Her body arched and strained, meeting him willingly, eagerly, aching for the ecstasy and fulfillment she'd only ever found in his arms.

Her hands gripped his shoulders, her fingers digging into his muscles, her nails scoring his skin. Her breath came in quick, shallow gasps as he drove her higher and higher to the pinnacle of their mutual pleasure.

Yes.

Please.

More.

And he gave her more. With his hands and his lips and his body, he gave and he gave until it was more than she could take. Pleasure poured through her, over her, a tidal wave of sensation that was so intense it stole her breath, her thoughts, her vision. There was nothing but bliss… and Jesse.

He was everything.

With a last thrust and a shudder, he collapsed on top of her, his face buried in the pillow beside her head.

She lifted a hand to his shoulder, let it trail down his back. His deliciously sculpted and tightly muscled body was truly a woman's fantasy—and he'd proven more than capable of satisfying every one of her fantasies, even the ones she hadn't realized that she had.

He lifted his weight off her, shifted so that he was beside her. But he kept his arm around her, holding her close. "Are you okay?" he asked.

Her lips curved. "I'm very okay."

He pulled her closer, so that her back was snug against his front and her head was tucked beneath his chin. "I almost forgot how good it was between us."

"I tried to convince myself it couldn't have been as good as I remembered." It was somehow easier to make the admission without looking at him. "But I was wrong."

"I missed you, Maggie."

"I missed you, too. But this…chemistry," she decided, for lack of a better term, "between us doesn't really change anything."

"You don't think so?"

"Wanting you—and wanting to be with you—doesn't alter the fact that our lives are twelve hundred miles apart."

"We'll figure it out," he told her.

He made it sound so easy, but Maggie knew there wasn't a simple answer. His suggestion that they should get married and raise their baby together wasn't a viable one. She couldn't—wouldn't—give up her career and her life in LA simply because he wanted to be a hands-on parent to their child. She admired his willingness to step up and respected his commitment to his ideals of fatherhood, but she was determined to focus on reality. And the reality was that her life, her family and her career were in California.

It wasn't likely that they were going to figure anything out—certainly not easily. She suspected it was more likely that there would be a lot of disagreement before any decisions were made, but it wasn't a battle she wanted to wage right now. Not while she was cradled in the warm strength of his arms, her body still sated from their lovemaking.

Within a few minutes, his breathing had evened out, and she knew he'd fallen asleep. As her own eyes started to drift shut, she found herself thinking about his impromptu offer of marriage. Not that she intended to accept—there were too many reasons to refuse, too many barriers to a relationship between them. But she couldn't deny that the prospect of sharing a bed with him for more than a few hours was undeniably tempting.

Chapter Four

When Jesse woke up, he was alone.

He could still smell Maggie's scent on his sheets, and there was an indent on the pillow where she'd slept, so he knew she couldn't have been gone long. He rose from his bed and moved to the window.

He didn't realize that his chest felt tight until he saw that her rental car was behind his truck in the driveway and the tension lessened. He'd been left with nothing more than a note on his kitchen table once before, and he didn't want to go through that again. He hadn't chased after Shaelyn—he'd had no interest in forcing her to stay in Rust Creek Falls when it was obvious she didn't want to be there.

But the situation with Maggie was different—she was carrying his baby, and that meant they had to figure out a way to work things out. If she had gone, he would have chased after her. He was glad he didn't have to.

He retrieved his jeans from the floor and tugged them on, then shoved his arms into the sleeves of his shirt and headed down the stairs. He found her standing at the stove, a spatula in her hand. The pressure in his chest eased a little more.

A glance at the numeric display on the stove revealed that it was after eight o'clock. "I guess we skipped dinner."

She looked up and offered a shy smile. "I hope you don't mind—I woke up hungry, and I thought you might be, too."

"I don't and I am," he told her. "French toast?"

"Is that okay?"

"Perfect."

She flipped the last piece of bread out of the frying pan and onto the plate, then carried the plate to the table, already set for two.

As she sat down across from him, he put a couple of slices on his plate, then liberally doused them with maple syrup. She took one slice, slowly ate it, cutting neat little squares that she dipped in a tiny puddle of syrup on her plate.

"I thought you said you were hungry."

"I was." She popped the last piece of toast into her mouth, then folded her napkin and set it on top of her plate. "And now I've eaten."

"You had one piece of French toast."

"I had two." One corner of her mouth tilted up in a half smile. "I ate the first one as soon as I flipped it out of the frying pan."

"Two whole slices?" He transferred another two to his own plate. "You must be stuffed."

"Don't make fun of me—I'm just happy to be able to keep down what I'm eating these days."

"I'm sorry," he said, sincerely contrite. "That must have been awful."

"It wasn't fun," she agreed.

"You should have called me."

She nodded. "I'm sorry I didn't."

He wanted to stay angry with her, but what was the point? Nothing could change what had happened since she left Rust Creek Falls in July, nothing could give them back the first four months of her pregnancy. But he couldn't help but think that, if she'd told him sooner, they might be in a different place right now.

Instead, he'd spent weeks dealing with the tangled emotions inside of him. He'd been hurt and angry and frustrated that he couldn't stop thinking about her. He'd tried to get over her—he'd even let his younger brother, Justin, set him up with a friend of the girl he was going out with. The date had been a complete bust, primarily because he couldn't stop thinking about Maggie. But recently he'd managed to convince himself that he was starting to forget about her—right up until the minute he saw her standing outside the paddock at Traub Stables.

"So," he began, thinking that a change of topic was in order, "things have been busy for you at work over the past couple of months?"

She nodded. "Busier than usual. Maybe too busy."

"Can you cut back on your hours?"

"Not if I want to keep my job."

"Do you?"

"Of course," she answered immediately, automatically.

Then her brow furrowed as she picked up her glass of water and sipped.

"Tell me about your new job," she finally suggested. "When I was here in the summer, you were working here, at your family's ranch, and now you're training horses."

"I still help out here, but it's the horses that have always been my focus."

"I heard they call you the horse whisperer in town—what exactly does that mean?"

"It's not as mystical as it sounds," he told her. "It just means that I don't use restraints or force when I'm training."

"How did you end up working at Traub Stables? I thought there was some long-standing feud between the Crawfords and the Traubs."

"There is," he acknowledged. "Although no one really

seems sure about its origins, whether it was a business deal gone bad or a romantic rivalry. Whatever the cause, I think my sister's marriage to Dallas Traub in February has helped build some bridges between the two families."

"So your family doesn't mind that you're working for Sutter Traub?"

His lips curved in a wry smile. "I wouldn't go that far," he acknowledged. "My father saw it as a betrayal. My mother warned that I was being set up—for what, she had no idea, but she was certain it was some kind of disaster in the making."

"Did you take the job despite their objections—or because of them?"

"Despite," he said. "I've wanted some space from my family for a long time, but that doesn't mean I don't love and respect them."

"And you don't mind that your boss is a Traub?"

"Sutter's a good guy who values the animals in his care and appreciates what I bring to his stables."

"I read a series of books when I was a kid, about a girl who lived on a ranch and raised an orphaned foal," she told him. "She fed it and trained it and entered riding competitions with it. After reading those books, I was desperate to experience the feeling of racing across open fields on horseback. I begged my parents to put me in a riding camp for the summer.

"They were always encouraging us to try new experiences, so they found a local camp and signed me up. I was so excited…until the first day. I'd never seen a horse up close until then," she confided. "And when we got to the Northbrook Riding Academy and I saw real, live horses galloping in the distance, I was terrified."

"What happened?" he asked, both curious about and grateful for this voluntary glimpse into her childhood.

"I begged to go home as passionately as I'd begged for the camp, but they made me stay. My parents are very big on commitment and follow-through. I was the one who wanted the experience, and they weren't going to let me quit."

"Did you ride?"

She shook her head. "The instructors tried to help me overcome my fear of the horses, but whenever I got too close, I would actually start to hyperventilate. Of course, the other kids made fun of me, which made the whole experience that much worse.

"Then I met Dolly. She was a white Shetland pony who was too old and lame to do much of anything, but she had the softest, kindest eyes.

"I spent most of the week with her. I brushed her and fed her and led her around her paddock. At the end of the week, I still hadn't been on the back of a horse, but I'd fallen in love with Dolly. For the next six months, I went back to Northbrook once a week just to visit her."

He didn't need to ask what had happened after six months. Considering that the pony had been old and lame, he was certain he knew. Instead he said, "Did you ever get over your fear of horses?"

"I haven't been around them much since that summer."

He pushed away from the table. "Get your coat and boots on."

"What? Why?"

"I want to introduce you to someone."

She shook her head. "I got over my childhood fascination with horses—I'm good now."

"Not if you're still afraid," he told her.

"I wouldn't say *afraid*," she denied. "More…cautious."

He took her coat from the hook, brought it over to her.

"I need to clean up the kitchen."

"The dishes will wait."

"Has anyone ever told you that you're pushy?"

He took her hand and guided it into the sleeve of her coat. "Not pushy—persuasive."

"I'm not feeling persuaded," she told him, but she put her other arm in her other sleeve. "My boots are still, um, upstairs."

In his bedroom, where he'd taken them off her along with the rest of her clothing before he'd made love with her.

"I'll get them," he said.

When he came back down, she had her coat zipped up to her chin, a hat on her head and a scarf wrapped around her throat.

He held back a smile as he knelt at her feet and helped her on with the boots. To someone who had lived her whole life in Southern California, Montana in November—even the first of November—was undoubtedly cold, but he knew it would be a lot colder in December, January and February.

He hoped she would be there to experience it.

Maggie could tell that Jesse was amused by her efforts to bundle up against the climate. As she carefully tucked her hands into woolen mittens, he stuffed his feet into his boots and tugged on a jacket, not even bothering to button it.

She stepped outside and gasped as the cold slapped her in the face and stole the breath from her lungs.

"It was seventy-two degrees when I left Los Angeles," she told him.

He slid an arm across her shoulders, holding her close to share body heat—of which he seemed to have an abundance. "The weather takes some getting used to for a lot of people."

She couldn't imagine ever getting used to the cold—or wanting to. Thankfully, the barn was only a short distance from his house, and she was grateful to duck into its warm shelter.

The facility was brightly lit and immaculate. The alleyway was interlocking brick and the wooden walls fairly gleamed. Jesse pulled the door closed and stood beside her, giving her a minute.

"Are you okay?" he asked gently.

She nodded, because she wanted it to be true, but she wasn't entirely certain. She'd heard that the olfactory sense was one of the strongest for evoking memories, but she'd never experienced it herself until she stepped inside the barn and breathed in the scent of hay and horses. Suddenly her brain was flooded with memories of that long-ago summer camp, and with the memories came apprehension and anxiety.

"Just breathe," he said.

It was only then that she realized she'd been holding her breath. She let it out now, and drew fresh air into her lungs. But that fresh air carried the same scent, and made her heart pound hard and fast inside her chest. "I feel stupid."

"Why?"

"Because I'm scared," she admitted.

"I won't let anything bad happen to you," he promised.

"It's late," she said. "I should get back before Lissa starts worrying."

He took her hands, holding her in place. "Do you trust me?"

She nodded without hesitation.

"So let's just stand right here for a minute until you relax."

"I'm not going to relax in here."

"You just need to focus on something other than the horses," he said.

And then, before she could assure him there was absolutely nothing that would take her focus off the enormous beasts behind the flimsy wooden doors, his lips were on hers. And within half a second, her mind went completely, blissfully blank.

He released the hands he'd been holding to wrap his arms around her, pulling her closer. Then his hands slid up her back, and even through the thick layers of clothing, she could feel the warmth of his touch. Or maybe the heat was all in her veins, stoked by his caress. His tongue traced the curve of her bottom lip, teasing, coaxing. Her mouth parted on a sigh, not just allowing him to deepen the kiss, but demanding it, as her tongue danced in a slow and seductive rhythm with his.

Her blood was pumping and her head was spinning as she gave herself over to the pleasure of his kiss. She could still smell hay and horses, but mixed in with those scents was the essence of Jesse. His heat, his strength, his heart.

He eased his mouth from hers, but continued to hold her close as they each took a moment to catch their breath.

"What are you thinking about now?" he asked.

"That I won't ever be able to walk into a barn without thinking about you and remembering this moment."

He smiled. "Good."

"My heart's still racing."

"But not because you're afraid," he guessed.

"No." She blew out a breath and tipped back her head to meet his gaze. "Is that your usual method for helping people overcome their apprehensions?"

"It's not one I've ever used before," he told her.

Her brows lifted. "So I was a guinea pig?"

"No, you're the woman who makes me forget all thought and reason."

The words, and the sincerity in his tone, mollified her.

"But I haven't forgotten why we came out here," he said, looping his arm around her waist and gently guiding her along the alleyway.

They'd moved only about six feet when a huge head appeared over the top of the door of the closest stall. She let out a squeak and immediately jumped back.

Jesse's arms came around her, holding her steady. He didn't force her to move any closer, but he didn't let her back any farther away, either.

"This is Honey," he told her. "And she is as sweet as her name."

"She's…beautiful," Maggie realized. The animal had a sleek chestnut coat that gleamed in the light, a white blaze, glossy mane and tail and eyes the color of melted chocolate. "And…big."

The horse tossed her head, almost as if she was nodding, and Maggie couldn't help but smile.

Jesse chuckled softly, and she felt the warmth of his breath on the back of her neck.

"Do you see how her ears are turned forward?"

She nodded.

"That shows that she's relaxed and paying attention to you."

"Is she hungry?"

He chuckled again. "No, she's had her dinner," he promised, reaching around Maggie to tug her mittens off. Then he took her hand and guided it toward the horse's long muzzle.

She felt herself start to tremble and had to fight against the urge to snatch her hand away.

"Steady," he murmured.

The mare watched her, its huge, liquid eyes patient and trusting. With Jesse's guidance, she stroked the smooth hair of its blaze. Honey blew out a breath— an equine sigh of contentment—and Maggie fell in love.

"Now I really wish I'd learned to ride," she admitted.

"I could teach you," Jesse said. "Not now, obviously. But after."

After.

The word seemed to hang in the air for a long minute, teasing her with possibilities. Neither of them knew what would happen *after*—they didn't even know what the next five months would hold, but she couldn't deny that she liked the idea of *after*.

"I think I'd enjoy that," she finally said.

"What are the rest of your plans for the weekend?" Jesse asked Maggie, as they made their way back to the house.

"I didn't really have any other plans," she told him. "I came to Rust Creek Falls to tell you about the baby, and I've done that."

"Maybe we could spend some more time together," he suggested. "Get to know one another a little better before we bring a baby into the world."

"That baby's coming in another five months whether we know one another or not," she pointed out.

"Then we shouldn't waste any time."

"What did you have in mind?"

"Nothing too crazy," he assured her, opening the back door to lead her into the house. "Maybe a drive up to Owl Rock to see the falls or a walk through town. Dinner at my parents' house."

"I'm sorry—what was that last part?"

"Dinner at my parents' house," he said again.

"You want me to meet your parents?"

"And I want them to meet the mother of their grand-child."

She blew out a breath. "I didn't think about the fact that our baby will have a lot more family in Rust Creek Falls than a daddy."

"We don't have to tell the grandparents-to-be right away. I just thought it might be nice if they had a chance to meet you before I told them that I got you pregnant."

"I guess that's reasonable," she allowed.

"We don't even have to spend a lot of time with them," he promised. "In fact, I'd prefer if we didn't."

She smiled at that. "Are you trying to talk me into—or out of—this?"

"I'm not sure."

"Okay, we'll have dinner with your parents."

"What about *your* parents?"

"It's a long way for them to come for dinner."

He managed a wry smile. "Don't you think I should meet them?"

"Maybe not," she teased. "Because they already know I'm pregnant."

"Then they should also know that I want to marry you."

"I thought we'd agreed that wasn't a good idea."

"You said it wasn't a good idea, then we spent some time together in bed, proving that it is, in fact, a very good idea."

"That is definitely my cue to be going."

"Or you could stay."

She shook her head. "If I stay, we're both going to start thinking that this is something it's not."

"What do you think it isn't?" he challenged.

"A relationship."

He hung his coat on a hook. "We've had sex, we're having a baby, but we don't have a relationship?"

"We've spent the past four months in different states,"

she reminded him. "Does that sound like a relationship to you?"

"Obviously it's a relationship that needs some work."

Her lips curved, but the smile didn't reach her eyes. "I don't want to give anyone—including you—the wrong idea about us."

"I appreciate that," he said. "But this isn't LA, and I think people around here will have an easier time accepting the fact that you're having my baby if they believe we were involved in a real relationship—even if it didn't work out."

"Is that the story you want to go with?"

"I'd rather give the real relationship part a chance—to see if we can make it work."

"Jesse—"

"Don't say no, Maggie. Not yet."

She sighed. "I'll see you tomorrow."

"I'll pick you up around ten."

"Actually, I have an appointment with Lissa in the morning," she told him. "Can I meet you here again?"

"Sure." He brushed a quick kiss over her lips. "Drive safe."

"I was about to send out the sheriff," Lissa said, when Maggie walked into the house twenty minutes later.

The sheriff was currently lounging on the sofa in front of the television, so Maggie waved to him. "Hi, Gage."

He lifted his hand to return the greeting. "I told you she wasn't eaten by bears," he admonished his wife.

"As if that was all I was worried about," Lissa muttered.

"Well, you can see that I'm safe and all in one piece," Maggie said.

"Hmm." Her cousin's gaze narrowed, as if she wasn't entirely convinced. "How did it go?"

"Better and worse than I expected."

"What's the 'better'?"

"He's not disputing that the baby's his."

"I should think not," Lissa said indignantly.

Maggie shook her head. "I haven't seen him since July—he wouldn't be human if he didn't ask questions."

"And the 'worse'?" her cousin prompted.

"He thinks we should get married."

"Oh. My. God." Lissa jumped up and hugged her. "This is sooo great."

"Obviously you got kicked in the head by the same horse that he did."

Gage chuckled; Lissa scowled at him.

"You don't think it would be great if Maggie married Jesse and moved to Rust Creek Falls?" she said to her husband.

"I think your cousin has a life—and a job—in LA that need to be taken into consideration," he countered reasonably.

"Thank you," Maggie said to him.

"But you could get a job here," Lissa implored. "Unlike LA, Rust Creek Falls isn't plagued by an abundance of lawyers."

"Now you sound like Jesse," Maggie grumbled.

"Just think about it," her cousin suggested.

"I will." The problem was, she really couldn't think straight when she was around Jesse. When she was with him, she wanted to believe that they could defy both the odds and geography and somehow make a relationship work.

But that had been the plan when she'd gone back to SoCal after the night they spent together in July. They were going to keep in touch and see one another whenever possible. Except that complications—in the form of her job and then her pregnancy—hadn't allowed it to be possible, and Jesse had grown tired of her excuses and the distance and stopped communicating with her.

Of course, there was more incentive now to make it work. But their baby wasn't a magical glue that could bond them together, nor should they expect him or her to be.

And if she was ever going to say yes to a marriage proposal, she wanted to be in love with the man who was asking. She just wasn't ready to admit to anyone—even her cousin and best friend—that she already was.

Chapter Five

"There's been a little snag to our plans," Jesse said, when Maggie showed up at his house just after 10:00 a.m. Saturday morning.

"What kind of snag?" she asked curiously.

He stepped away from the door so she could enter. When she did, she saw a baby girl standing at the coffee table.

The child had wispy blond hair, big blue eyes and was dressed in a pair of pink overalls. And there was something about her—the shape of her eyes, the tilt of her chin—that launched her stomach into her throat.

She swallowed, and managed to find her voice. "You already have a baby?"

"What? No." The shock in his voice was real. "This is Noelle—my niece."

"Oh." She exhaled an audible sigh of relief.

Jesse scrubbed a hand over his face as he let out a nervous laugh. "Don't you think I would have told you something like that?"

She would have thought so, but she really didn't know him that well. If she had, she might have known that he had a niece. "I just saw the baby and my mind started spinning," she admitted.

"I would have warned you—if I'd had any warning myself," he told her. "Dallas took the boys to Kalispell to see a movie and Nina had to fill in at the store at the last minute. Usually she would take the baby with her, but Noelle's teething and cranky and Nina was afraid she'd scare off the customers."

"She doesn't look cranky to me."

"Give her a few minutes," Jesse said drily, hanging Maggie's coat on a hook.

"Do you babysit very often?"

"No. Nina can usually handle everything on her own, and when she does need help, there's a lineup of volunteers, including her husband, stepsons, grandparents on both sides and numerous aunts and uncles. But no one else was available today, so Noelle was dumped in my lap."

Maggie sat on the storage bench by the door and untied her boots. "So this wasn't part of your plan? Because I have to admit—this kind of feels like a test."

"A test?"

"To see how badly I'm going to screw up as a mother."

"It's not a test," he assured her. "And you're not going to screw up."

On the table in front of the sofa was a small plastic bowl containing a few cereal O's, with more scattered on the table and the carpet. When Maggie sat down, the little girl shuffled sideways toward her, holding on to the table as she went. Then she looked up at Maggie with a wide, droolly smile that revealed four tiny white teeth.

"She's adorable."

"She is pretty cute," he agreed. "But don't tell my sister I said so."

"Why not?"

"Because Noelle looks just like Nina when she was a baby." He sat on the floor and began to stack up the wooden blocks that were scattered around.

Noelle put her hand on Maggie's thigh and uncurled

her fist to reveal a crumbly cereal O. She left it on Maggie's pants, like a present, before she plopped down on the floor and crawled over to see what her uncle was doing.

Jesse was on the fourth level of blocks when his niece reached out with both hands and pushed them over.

"Oopsie," he said, and the little girl clapped her hands and laughed gleefully.

Maggie watched them play the same game for several minutes, amused by the easy interaction between them. "You're so natural with her."

"She makes it easy," Jesse told her. "She's a good baby."

"I don't have a lot of experience with kids," she admitted.

"That will change fast," he told her.

Noelle moved from the blocks to a ball that lit up and played music when it was rolled. When she gave up on the toys and went back to her cereal, Jesse decided it was time to make lunch, and he left Maggie supervising the baby.

She decided that she could stack blocks, too, and she sat down on the floor to do so. But Noelle wasn't overly interested in the structure Maggie was building. Instead, she was scouring the carpet for lost pieces of cereal. Only when she'd found them all did she crawl over to investigate Maggie's construction efforts. Of course, the house tumbled down and Noelle laughed and clapped. Then she picked up one of the blocks and shoved one corner of it into her droolly mouth.

"I don't know if you're supposed to be eating that," Maggie said dubiously.

The little girl continued to gnaw on the corner of the wood.

"I know you're probably hungry, but Uncle Jesse's getting your lunch ready so you might want to save your appetite."

Noelle kept her gaze fixed on Maggie, as if fascinated by what she was saying. Her lips curved in recognition of *Uncle Jesse*, but she continued to chew on the block.

"Why don't you give me that?" Maggie suggested, reaching for the square of wood. "Then we can use it to build a castle for—"

That was as far as she got, because when she managed to gently pry the block from the little girl's hand, Noelle started to scream like a banshee.

Panicked, Maggie immediately gave the piece of wood back to her. The little girl snatched the cube from her hand and threw it—bouncing it off Maggie's cheekbone and bringing tears to *her* eyes.

"What the heck—?" Jesse asked, appearing from the other side of the couch.

"I took her block away," Maggie admitted.

"Why?"

"I've read stuff…about lead paint and chemicals in children's toys, and I didn't think she should be chewing on the blocks."

"There's no paint on those blocks," Jesse pointed out. "They were handmade by my grandfather for Nina when she was a baby." Then he seemed to notice the red welt on Maggie's cheek and winced. "She's got a good arm, doesn't she?"

Maggie just nodded.

"I'll be right back," he said.

Noelle, having recovered her favorite wooden cube, was gnawing happily again, her explosive outburst apparently forgotten.

Jesse returned a minute later with a baggie filled with frozen peas and laid it gently against Maggie's cheekbone. "How's that feel?"

"Cold."

He smiled. "How do you feel?"

"Ridiculous," she admitted.

"Hungry?" he prompted.

"Sure."

Lunch was remarkably uneventful. Jesse had made grilled cheese sandwiches and French fries for everyone. He cut the little girl's sandwich into bite-size pieces, gave her a few fries and added a spoonful of corn niblets to her plate.

"Because her mother doesn't consider potatoes in fried form to be a real vegetable," he explained to Maggie.

Before the meal was done, Noelle was yawning and rubbing her eyes with a fist.

"Someone looks ready for her bottle," Jesse noted.

"Ba-ba," his niece confirmed.

"Why don't you give Noelle her bottle and I'll clean up the kitchen?" Maggie suggested.

"KP being the lesser of two evils?" Jesse teased.

She felt her cheeks flush. "It just seems fair, since you cooked, that I do the cleanup."

"In that case, I'll take you up on your offer," he said, scooping up the baby with his free arm. "But I think diaper change before bottle, because this little princess looks ready for a nap."

While Jesse tackled the diaper change—no way was Maggie ready for *that* challenge—she filled the sink with soapy water.

As she washed up and then dried the dishes, she could hear Jesse talking to the baby while she drank her bottle, his tone quiet and soothing. But as she put the dishes away, she realized he'd been silent for a while now, and she suspected that the little girl had probably fallen asleep.

She folded the towel over the handle of the oven and wandered into the living room.

She was right—the baby was asleep. So was Jesse.

And something about the image of the big strong man with the beautiful baby girl in his arms made her heart completely melt. There was absolutely no doubt that he loved his sister's child—or that he was going to be a fabulous father to their baby. She only wished she could be half as confident about her own parenting abilities.

Maggie touched a hand to her belly and thought of the tiny life growing inside her womb, suddenly assailed with doubts about her ability to meet all of her baby's needs, to be the mother her child deserved.

Noelle's mother worked full-time, but she was able to take her baby to work with her and she had family who were willing and able to help out with the baby as needed. Those same options weren't available to Maggie. Even if there was room in her shared office for a playpen—and there wasn't—she couldn't imagine the partners would ever approve that arrangement.

As for her family, she knew her parents would help in any way that they could, but they both had demanding careers of their own. And because she was at the start of hers, Maggie worked an average of ten hours a day, six days a week. Who would take care of her baby for all of that time?

Despite the size of the firm, there was no on-site day care at Alliston & Blake. Of course, most of the female lawyers on staff were primarily focused on their careers. She knew a few of them had children: Deirdre McNichol had three kids, but she also had a husband who was a playwright and able to work at home with their children; Lynda Simmons had invited her mother to move in so that she could look after her grandchild while Lynda was working; and Candace Hartman had a nanny—of course, she was a partner, so she could afford to pay someone to come into her house to take care of her child. Obviously none of those options was viable for Maggie, so she'd have to figure out something that was.

But first, she had to face dinner with Jesse's parents.

Dinner at the Crawfords' was always an experience—and probably not one that Jesse should have subjected Maggie to just yet. And definitely not while he was still hoping to convince her to marry him.

No one had ever accused his parents of being subtle, and as soon as Maggie sat down across from Jesse at the dinner table, the interrogation began. From "Where do you live in California?" and "What brings you to Rust Creek Falls this weekend?" to "How did you meet Jesse?" and everything in between.

No subject was off-limits, as his father proved when he asked, "What do you think about a woman planning to have a baby out of wedlock?"

Not surprisingly, the question made Maggie choke on her water.

"Really, Todd," his wife chided. "That's hardly appropriate dinner conversation." Which suggested that she at least had some boundaries, although Jesse didn't really believe it.

In an effort to divert the focus away from Maggie, he chimed in. "There are a lot of women who pursue nontraditional options to satisfy their desire for a family," he said, in a direct quote of the explanation his sister had once given to him.

"Nontraditional options," his father sputtered. "Nina got knocked up by some stranger through a turkey baster."

"Now she has a beautiful baby girl," his wife said soothingly. "*And* a husband."

"And three more kids she didn't plan on having," Todd noted.

"Three wonderful boys, who are now our grandchildren, too," Laura agreed. "And if we're lucky, Nate and Callie won't wait too much longer to give us even more."

"Give them time," her husband urged. "They're not even married yet."

"But they're so perfectly suited," Laura said. Then she turned to Maggie and said, in a confidential tone, "I had some concerns at first. There was a whole group of women who came here after the big flood last year, each one of them looking to hook up with a cowboy, and when Callie set her sights on Nate—as she did from the get-go—I was afraid she was just like them. Some of those women don't understand the life of a rancher—it isn't nearly as romantic as it looks in books and movies."

"Nothing ever is," Maggie agreed.

"But the important thing is that Callie and Nate are happy together." Laura paused to glance at her son. "We just hope Jesse will find someone who suits him so perfectly someday."

The implication being, of course, that Maggie couldn't be that someone. And though she kept a polite smile on her face, Jesse knew that his mother's remark had not been lost on her.

But still his mother had to hammer the point home, as she did when she asked, "So when are you going back to California?"

"Tomorrow," Maggie admitted.

"Well, I hope you'll stop by again the next time you're in town. Whenever that might be."

It was a dismissal—and not even a polite one. But he should have realized that Maggie wasn't the type of woman to let herself be dismissed, and while he was trying to figure out what he could say to clarify the situation, she responded.

"I'm sure it will be soon," Maggie said, matching his mother's cool tone. "We've got a lot to figure out before the baby comes."

Laura's fake smile froze on her face.

Todd turned to Maggie, his thick brows drawn together in a thunderous scowl. "You're pregnant?"

She nodded. "But don't worry—there were no turkey basters involved. I got knocked up the old-fashioned way."

Jesse hadn't intended to share the news of his impending parenthood with his own parents just yet, because he knew what they would expect him to do—it was the same thing he expected of himself: to marry the mother-to-be and give their child a family. And while he knew he wouldn't be able to keep Maggie's pregnancy a secret for much longer, he hadn't been anxious to go another round with his parents.

Their relationship had hit a serious snag when he'd told his mom and dad that he'd been offered a job at Traub Stables and they'd forbidden him to accept it. Forbidden him—as if he was a teenager rather than a twenty-nine-year-old man.

So while he hadn't planned to tell them about the baby, he couldn't regret that Maggie had done so—especially when her announcement had actually struck his mother mute for a whole three minutes.

"I can't believe I said that. To your parents." She dropped her face into her hands as they drove away from The Shooting Star. "I'm a horrible person."

"You were magnificent," he told her.

She shook her head. "Your mother pushed all of my buttons."

"She has a knack for that."

"I shouldn't have let her push my buttons. I should have just smiled and kept my mouth shut."

"I'm glad you didn't."

"Now they hate me."

"They don't hate you."

"They hate me," she said again. "And yet, they still expect you to marry me. How screwed up is that?"

He shrugged. "My family's big on taking responsibility."

"I thought they were big on finding someone who would suit you 'so perfectly.'"

"Apparently a baby trumps everything else."

"At least I understand a little better now why you felt compelled to propose."

He turned into the Christensens' driveway. "I do agree that a baby should have two parents."

"We've been through this once already tonight," she reminded him.

"But you still haven't agreed to marry me."

"Because I'm a big-city liberal who isn't morally opposed to nontraditional families."

"I'm not, either," he said. "Except when it comes to my child."

"Our lives aren't just in different cities but different states," she reminded him.

A fact of which he was painfully aware. And he didn't know what he could say or do to convince her to give them a chance to build a life together; he didn't have any new arguments to make. So he reiterated the most important one: "Our baby needs both of us."

He parked the truck in front of the sheriff's house, and although she was reaching for the handle before he'd turned off the engine, he scooted out of the vehicle and around the passenger side to help her out.

"There's no doubt your parents raised you to be a gentleman."

He lifted a finger to tip back the brim of his hat. "Yes, ma'am," he said, and made her smile.

But her smile quickly faded. "I wish I could say yes."

His heart bumped against his ribs. "It's a simple word—just three little letters."

"Those three little letters can't miraculously span twelve hundred miles." She started toward the house, and he fell into step beside her.

"We can figure it out," he said, desperately hoping it was true.

"I'm going back tomorrow," she reminded him. "I've got an early flight."

He sighed. "Will you let me drive you to the airport?"

She shook her head. "I've got to return my rental car, anyway."

"Can I call you?"

"Of course."

He caught her hand as she reached the door. "I know you have a lot to think about, but let me add just one more thing to the list," he said.

And then he kissed her.

Maggie didn't like to leave her car in the airport parking lot if she didn't have to, and she usually managed to cajole her brother Ryan into playing taxi driver. But when she got off the plane Sunday afternoon, she discovered that he'd somehow talked their mother into doing the pickup.

And when she saw Christa, Maggie felt her throat tighten and her eyes fill with tears. It both baffled and frustrated her that she could keep her chin up in the face of almost any kind of adversity, but as soon as she saw her mother, all of her defenses toppled and she felt like a little girl in need of her comforting embrace.

Christa, sensing that need, instinctively opened her arms and drew Maggie into them.

"What story did Ryan concoct to get out of airport duty this time?"

"There was no story," Christa said. "I volunteered."

"You hate driving around the airport."

Her mother shrugged. "I thought you might want to talk."

"I do," she agreed. "I just don't have the first clue where to begin."

Christa didn't press her. In fact, she didn't say anything else until they were in the car and driving away from the airport—except to ask for directions.

Once they were on the highway, Maggie finally vocalized the question that had been hovering at the back of her mind. "How did you manage to juggle a legal career and three kids?"

"I'd be lying if I said it was easy," Christa told her. "And I'm not sure I could have done it when you were babies."

"You weren't working then?"

Her mother shook her head. "I took a leave of absence when we adopted Shane and didn't go back to work full-time until you were in kindergarten."

"You took twelve years off?" She guessed at the number, since it was the age difference between herself and her oldest brother.

"It was actually closer to sixteen, although I did work a few hours a week at Legal Aid, to keep my hand in," her mother explained. "But your dad and I both agreed that if we were going to have children, our children needed to be a priority. I didn't want to work to pay someone else to raise you.

"That's not a choice every woman can make," she acknowledged, "but I was lucky to have your dad's support in that decision."

"I don't want to give up my career," Maggie said. "But I don't want to be so wrapped up in my career that I miss out on being a mother to my child."

"You don't have to choose one or the other," her mother pointed out.

"I'm not sure Brian Nash would say the same thing."

"Then maybe you need a new boss."

"I've dedicated almost half a decade to Alliston & Blake."

"Yes, you have," Christa agreed.

And Maggie heard what she didn't say—that maybe the time she'd already given them was enough. But leaving Alliston & Blake, trying something new and different, was a scary prospect. A little bit exciting but mostly scary, especially now that she had more than her career to think about—she had a baby on the way.

"I don't know what's the right thing to do," she admitted. "I know how to research precedent and draft motions and argue cases—I don't know how to be a mother."

"Being a parent is the toughest job you'll ever have, and the most important."

"What if I screw up?"

"You will," her mother said easily. "Every mother does once in a while. Every father, too."

"That was subtle, Mom."

Christa smiled. "I wasn't trying to be subtle."

"If you have questions about the baby's father, why don't you just ask them?"

"I don't have any specific questions—I just want you to tell me something about him. There was a time when you used to tell me everything about the boys you liked, but you've been awfully closemouthed since your trip to Montana in the summer."

Maggie wondered if it was possible to sum up Jesse in a handful of words, if there was any way to describe the way she felt when she was with him, any way to explain the conflicting emotions that she didn't understand.

"His name is Jesse Crawford," she said, deciding to start with the simple facts. "His family owns the general store in Rust Creek Falls and The Shooting Star ranch, but Jesse trains horses."

"So he's a cowboy," Christa mused.

Maggie nodded. "He's strong and smart, a little bit shy but incredibly sexy. There's an intensity about him, a single-minded focus. And he has a real gift for working with animals. They respond to him—his hands and his voice."

"I'm thinking he has the same gift with women," her mother noted drily.

Maggie felt her cheeks flush. "Maybe. But Lissa assured me he doesn't have that kind of reputation. In fact, since she's been living in Rust Creek Falls, she hasn't heard of him dating anyone at all."

"So what brought the two of you together?"

"Happenstance? Luck? Fate?"

Her mother's immaculately arched brows lifted. "Fate?"

"Something just clicked between us when we met," she said. "It was almost like…magic. I know that sounds corny, but I can't explain it any better than that."

"You're in love with him," Christa realized.

"I think…maybe…I am," she agreed hesitantly. "But is that even possible? I only met him a few months ago, I haven't spent that much time with him and I don't know him that well. But there's this almost magnetic draw that I can't seem to resist—that I don't want to resist when I'm with him."

"Have you told him how you feel?"

She shook her head.

"Why not?"

"Because I don't know how he feels."

"Love shouldn't be given with strings—it's a gift from the heart."

"Even if I told him, even if he—by some miracle—felt the same way, it doesn't really change anything."

"Honey, love changes everything."

"Maybe that's what makes me uneasy," Maggie finally admitted. "I like my life the way it is—and I get that having a baby will require some changes. But since I told Jesse, he's suddenly gone all Neanderthal, insisting that we should get married."

"You don't sound very happy about that."

"I'd be happy if I thought he wanted to spend the rest of his life with me," she admitted, startled to realize it was true.

"Isn't that usually the motivating factor behind a proposal?"

"The motivating factor for Jesse is our baby."

"Are you sure about that?" her mother asked gently.

"I told him I was pregnant and he said 'we should get married.'"

"And what did you say?"

"I said no."

"Did he accept that?"

"No," she admitted.

Christa smiled. "When do we get to meet him?"

Chapter Six

Since Jesse couldn't leave his animals unattended for a weekend, he called his brother Brad and asked him to take care of them. Of course, his brother showed up Friday just as Jesse was getting ready to head out.

"So where are you going this weekend?" he asked curiously.

"Los Angeles."

"California?"

"No, Los Angeles, Montana."

"Okay, it was a stupid question," Brad allowed. "But why are you going to California?"

"To see Maggie."

His brother narrowed his gaze. "That lawyer you were all ga-ga over in the summer?"

"No one over the age of twelve uses the expression *ga-ga*," Jesse chided. "But yes, Maggie is an attorney."

"I didn't even know you were dating her."

No one knew they were dating—because they weren't. But they were having a baby together and although his parents were now aware of that fact, they'd been surprisingly closemouthed about the situation. Probably because they were waiting for him to announce a wedding date, which he didn't think was going to happen anytime soon.

While he knew that Maggie's pregnancy couldn't remain a secret forever—and probably not very much longer—he wasn't ready to share the news with Brad. So he decided to go with the same explanation that Maggie had given to Jared Winfree. "We wanted to keep our relationship under the radar, to avoid small-town gossip."

"You definitely did that," Brad allowed. "I guess it's pretty serious, though, if you're going to LA to see her."

"I want to marry her," Jesse admitted.

His brother shook his head. "Why would you want to tie yourself to one woman when there are so many of them out there? And if you insist on settling down, why wouldn't you choose a local girl? Why would you hook up with another big-city gal who's only going to break your heart?"

"Thanks for the vote of confidence," Jesse said drily.

"You were devastated when Shaelyn left," Brad reminded him. "I don't want you to go through something like that again."

Actually, he'd been more relieved than devastated, having realized even before Shaelyn did that their engagement had been a mistake. But he didn't argue the point with his brother because Brad was right about one thing—Maggie was a big-city gal and it was entirely possible that he was making a big mistake.

Again.

Busy. Crowded. Frantic.

Those were Jesse's first impressions of Los Angeles, and that was before he left the airport terminal.

Thankfully everything he'd needed had fit into a carry-on, so he didn't have to battle the mass of people at baggage claim. He weaved through the crowd, feeling like a salmon swimming upstream. Or maybe the more appropriate analogy would be like a fish out of water.

Except that when he finally spotted Maggie, everything and everyone else seemed to fade away.

She offered him a quick smile and a kiss on the cheek. "Is that everything?" she asked, indicating the duffel bag slung over his shoulder.

"That's everything," he confirmed.

She nodded and led him toward the exit. "I got caught up in a meeting and didn't have a chance to pick up a file that I need this weekend. Do you mind if I make a quick stop at the office now?"

"Of course not," he said. In fact, he was curious to see where she worked—the big-city lawyer in her natural milieu.

But that was before she pulled out of the airport parking lot and onto the highway and he realized that Los Angeles traffic was insane. He'd never experienced anything like it and was beyond grateful that he didn't have to drive in it. And when Maggie began to zip from lane to lane, he just closed his eyes and held on.

They arrived at the offices of Alliston & Blake twenty minutes later. Maggie pulled into an underground parking garage and led him from there to a bank of elevators. She punched the call button for the one designated Floors 10–21, and once inside, they began the ascent toward the eighteenth floor.

"Are you okay?" she asked. "You look a little pale."

"I think so," he said. "I'd heard about California traffic, but I didn't anticipate anything quite like that."

"That was nothing compared to rush hour," she told him.

"I'll happily skip that experience, if it's an option."

She smiled. "I'll try to get in and out as quickly as possible."

He followed her into a small office with two desks and the same number of filing cabinets and bookcases. She went to the closer desk, the one with a neatly engraved nameplate that said Maggie Roarke. A similar nameplate on the other desk said Samantha Radke.

Maggie must have noted the direction of his gaze, because she said, "Sammi's working out of the San Francisco office this week."

While she sifted through a neat stack of folders, he moved farther into the room, checking out the diplomas on the wall and noting the summa cum laude designation on Maggie's certificate from Stanford Law.

"Got it," she said, just as a brisk knock sounded on the open door, immediately followed by a man's voice, "Good—you're back."

Maggie's smile froze on her face. "And on my way out again, Brian."

The man—Brian—didn't seem pleased by her response. And that was before he spotted Jesse standing beside her desk.

"Who's the cowboy?" he asked, speaking to Maggie as if Jesse wasn't even in the room.

"Jesse is…a friend of mine," she said. "Jesse Crawford. Brian Nash."

His hands were soft, his grip weak. The suit was obviously a pencil pusher who wouldn't be able to wrestle a fifty-pound sack of grain never mind a two-thousand-pound bull. Which didn't surprise Jesse or concern him—but he didn't like the way the other man put his hand on Maggie's shoulder, then let it linger there.

"I'm glad I caught you," Brian was saying to her now. "I have a meeting with Perry Edler tonight that I thought you might want to attend."

Perry Edler—the Chief Operating Officer of Edler Industries, one of Alliston & Blake's biggest clients. The invitation—and the possibilities that it implied—made Maggie's pulse quicken. Then she glanced from Brian to

Jesse, and her pulse quickened again, but for an entirely different reason.

"Tonight?" She shook her head with sincere regret. "I can't."

Brian frowned. "What do you mean—you can't?"

She couldn't blame him for sounding confused. In the almost five years that she'd worked at Alliston & Blake, she had probably never before uttered those same words. Her job had always been her number one priority and she'd happily juggled every other part of her life to accommodate it.

"I'm sorry," she apologized automatically. "But I already have plans for tonight."

"Plans?" Her boss's frown deepened as his gaze skipped to Jesse again. "Plans can't compare to opportunities, and this is an incredible opportunity for you, Maggie. Mr. Edler specifically asked that you be assigned to his team for this new project."

She looked at Jesse, her conviction wavering. His expression was guarded, giving her no hint of what he was thinking or feeling. He was leaving the choice entirely up to her, and she knew that if she told him this meeting was more important than their dinner plans because it had the potential to make her career, he'd probably wish her luck.

But was it?

Was one meeting with Perry Edler more important than the conversation she needed to have with her baby's father—a conversation for which he'd traveled more than twelve hundred miles?

Maybe the answer to that question should have been immediately obvious to her, but it wasn't. Because her job wasn't just important—it was vital. If she didn't have her job at Alliston & Blake, she'd have no income to provide the essentials of life—food, clothing, shelter—for her baby.

And okay, working as an attorney she'd have to add day care to that list, and day care was expensive, which meant that she'd have to increase her billable hours, which meant working more hours. The cycle was endless, and it made her head ache just to think about it.

If she let this one client meeting take precedence, where would it end? When would her job stop being more important than her life? When would the needs of her child finally matter more than the demands of her boss?

Brian took her silence as acquiescence. "We have an eight o'clock reservation at Patina—I'll see you there."

She looked at Jesse. "Can you give us a minute, please?"

"Sure," he agreed easily, already moving toward the door with the long, loose stride that was somehow both easy and sexy.

She waited until he'd closed the door before she turned back to her boss. "I'm sorry," she said again, but more firmly this time. "I can't make it."

His brows lifted. "This is a major career opportunity, Maggie."

She knew that it was—but she didn't much care for the strings that were obviously attached. "For the past five years, I've done everything you've asked of me— and more. I've come in early and stayed late. I've worked weekends and holidays that no one else wanted to work."

"And that's why you've earned this opportunity," he confirmed. "But if you're unavailable tonight, I'm sure Patricia will be pleased to join Mr. Edler's group."

Patricia was another junior associate who had made no secret of her ambitions—or her willingness to step on other people as she climbed her way to the top at Alliston & Blake.

"I thought Mr. Edler specifically asked for me."

"He asked for a young up-and-comer with lots of energy and enthusiasm." Brian amended his earlier claim. "I thought that was you."

"And now it's Patricia," she realized dully.

"You're good, but you're not indispensable," her boss said.

"I see."

"Do you?"

She was afraid that she did. And she was angry and frustrated because she knew there was nothing she could do—notwithstanding everything that she'd already done—to sway his opinion. If she couldn't be available to the firm every minute of every day, he would find someone who could.

She glanced from her boss to the door through which Jesse had exited. She could see him through the glass, leaning on a horizontal filing cabinet and chatting to one of the secretaries. Brian was a company man, from his neatly styled salon-trimmed hair to his immaculately polished Italian leather shoes. Jesse was every inch a cowboy—with a capital *C*. He was rugged and rough, charming and sweet, and he'd crossed state lines to be with her this weekend.

She'd never known anyone like him and it was immediately evident to her why—because he didn't, and wouldn't ever, fit in her corporate world.

Brian, obviously having followed the direction of her gaze, lifted his brows. "Do you really want to throw away this opportunity for some cowboy that you're having a fling with?"

"We're not having a fling," she told him. "We're having a baby."

He frowned. "You're joking."

"Actually, I'm not."

"You're really pregnant?"

She nodded. "Due in April."

"Well, that puts a different spin on the situation."

"Why is that?"

"As you already noted, I need someone who is available to come in early and stay late, someone who can work weekends and holidays. Are you still going to be able to do that when you have a baby at home?"

"I don't know," she admitted.

"That's not an answer that's going to get you very far in this firm," he warned.

"Are you firing me?"

"No," he said quickly. "Of course not. You're a valued associate and an important member of the Alliston & Blake team."

Which only meant that he knew he couldn't fire her without risk of being sued for unlawful termination.

"And I won't ever be anything more than an associate here, will I?"

"You know that's not my decision to make."

"You're a partner, Brian—one of the most senior, aside from Mr. Alliston and Mr. Blake. When you make a recommendation, the rest of the partners listen."

"If you're asking if I would recommend you for the partner track, I would have to say that, right now, I would not."

Though it was the answer she'd anticipated, it was still a shock to hear him say the words aloud. "That's not fair."

He shrugged. "It's a fact of life, Maggie. A partner is expected to put the needs of the firm first. Always."

"I can, and I would," she said, although without much conviction.

"Tell me," Brian said, "what you would do if you were on your way to court for closing arguments in a trial and the day care called because your child was feverish and vomiting?"

She didn't say anything, because she knew the answer

she would give him wasn't the answer he wanted to hear. And he knew it, too.

"Being a mother is a noble undertaking, but not one that's compatible with a partnership at Alliston & Blake."

Maggie dropped the file she'd come into the office to retrieve back on top of her desk.

"I'll see you on Monday."

Maggie didn't say anything to Jesse about her conversation with Brian. She didn't want him to feel sorry for her; she didn't want to give him any ammunition to manipulate her emotions to his own purposes; but mostly she didn't want his empathy, because she was afraid that would be her undoing.

"Do you like sushi?" she asked, when they exited the building.

He made a face. "No, and you shouldn't eat it, either, while you're pregnant."

"Suddenly you're an expert on pregnancy?"

"I've been reading up, learning a few things."

"Can I have steak?"

He nodded, either oblivious to or ignoring the sarcasm in her tone. "Red meat has lots of protein and iron, but it should be thoroughly cooked to ensure there is no residual bacteria."

"You really have been reading up," she noted, feeling duly chastised.

"I'm interested," he said simply.

She was, too, and she'd gone out to buy all of the best-reviewed books when her doctor had confirmed that she was going to have a baby. But they were still in a neat pile on her bedside table because she was usually too tired when she got home at the end of the day to want to crack the cover of a pregnancy guide or child-care manual.

"I'm hungry," she said, and led him through a set of frosted glass doors and into Lou's Chophouse.

The atmosphere was upscale casual, the decor consisting of glossy wood tables and leather-padded benches, with frosted glass dividers separating the booths and pendant-style lights hanging over the tables. When they were seated, the hostess handed them menus in leather folders, ran through the daily specials and promised that their server would be over momentarily to take their drink order.

Maggie ordered the peppercorn sirloin with basmati rice and steamed broccoli. He opted for the twelve-ounce strip loin with a fully loaded baked potato and seasonal vegetables.

But when her meal was delivered, she found she had no appetite. Mindful of the tiny life in her belly, though, she forced herself to cut into the steak and eat a few bites.

She didn't fool Jesse. He was halfway through his own steak when he said, "You're picking at your food."

"I guess I'm not as hungry as I thought I was."

"Is that all it is?"

She stabbed at her broccoli. "No," she admitted. "But I don't want to talk about it."

"Have you changed your mind?"

"About what?"

"Keeping the baby."

"No," she answered without hesitation. "I'm not sure about a lot of things, but I'm sure about that."

He exhaled an audible sigh of relief. "You probably know there aren't a lot of lawyers in Rust Creek Falls. In fact, Ben Dalton is it, but word around town is that he's interested in bringing in an associate."

"I have a job," she reminded him.

"I'm just presenting you with another option."

"Except that it's not an option, because I'm not licensed to practice in Montana."

"You'd have to pass the State Bar," he acknowledged.

"Have you been reading up on that, too?"

"A little."

"Then you should know that writing a Bar exam is a little more complicated than going to the store to pick up a quart of milk."

"Do you think the Montana exam is more difficult than the one you wrote here?"

"No," she admitted. "But I wrote the California Bar five years ago."

"And you've forgotten how to study since then?"

One side of her mouth tipped up in response to his teasing. "I don't think so."

"Then it's something you could at least consider?"

"Yes, it's something I could consider," she agreed. "But if I did get a job in Rust Creek Falls, what would I do about day care?"

"We have day care in Montana. In fact, the Country Kids Day Care is just a few blocks from Ben Dalton's office."

"Why are you okay with me putting our baby in day care in Rust Creek Falls but not in LA?"

"Because you wouldn't need day care for twelve hours a day," he pointed out logically. "Because even if you had to work late, I'd bc there to help out, so our child would have more time with both parents."

"You make it sound so logical."

"It *is* logical."

She sighed. "I used to have a plan for my life and confidence that I knew exactly what I was doing. Now...I don't have a clue."

"So we'll figure it out together," he said.

"And what if we don't?"

"When you walk into a courtroom, do you worry that you can't handle the case?"

"I never walk into a courtroom unprepared."

"Exactly."

"I'm not sure the same rules apply to pregnancy and parenthood."

"I'm not sure there are any rules for parenthood—more like guidelines."

"Thanks, Captain Barbossa."

He grinned, pleased that she'd recognized the movie reference.

Maggie just sighed. "I used to be able to think things through—now my emotions seem to be all over the map, and I don't know if that's just the pregnancy hormones or..."

"Or?" he prompted.

"Or maybe this baby is giving me the excuse I need to make the changes to my life that I've wanted to make for a while."

"I have an idea for a change," he said. "You could marry me."

She shook her head.

"Why not?"

"Because I'm trying to be rational," she reminded him.

"You're pregnant with my baby, we have good chemistry—which might explain the baby," he acknowledged, earning a small smile from her. "You like to cook, I like to eat."

"Wow, your argument is...underwhelming."

"I'll be faithful, Maggie. I can promise you that." He knew it wasn't a declaration likely to make a woman swoon, but it was honest.

"I'm not sure that should be enough for either of us," she said softly.

"I'm not looking to fall in love."

"Why not?"

"Can we focus on what's relevant here?"

"What do you consider relevant?" she asked.

"The fact that I want to be a husband to you and a father to our baby." He reached across the table and covered her hand with his. "And maybe give that baby a brother or a sister someday."

"How do you know you want to be a husband to me?" she challenged. "You don't even know me."

"I know that you're beautiful and smart and warm and compassionate. I know that your family is important to you. You're close to your parents and your brothers and our baby is a real, biological connection to me and will bind us together forever.

"I know you enjoy your work, and I don't think you'd be happy to give up your career. But I also don't think you'll be happy, long-term, in a career that takes everything from you and gives nothing back—as it seems your job at Alliston & Blake is doing.

"The fact that you want to have and keep this baby proves you want to be a mother, and since you don't do anything in half measures, you want to be a good mother. Which means that you need to find a way to balance work outside the home with responsibilities to the child that we're bringing into the world."

She didn't know if anyone had seen into her heart so clearly, and the realization that he'd done so was a little worrisome. If he could read her thoughts and feelings that easily, it wouldn't take him long to figure out that she had strong feelings for him, and she was afraid he would manipulate those feelings to get what he wanted.

"You missed one thing," she told him.

"What's that?"

"I was raised by two parents who love one another as much as they love their children, and I always promised myself that if and when I did get married, it would be because I'd found someone that I loved the same way."

"I'd say the baby you're carrying trumps that idealistic dream."

Idealistic dream.

The dismissal in those two words cut to the quick. Just when she'd almost been ready to let him persuade her that they could make a marriage work, those two words told her so much more than he'd likely intended.

"She must have really done a number on you," Maggie mused.

"Who?"

"The woman who made you afraid to risk your heart."

Chapter Seven

Jesse didn't want to talk about the past but the future— his future with Maggie and their baby.

Except that her insight, as uncomfortable as it made him, was valid. And it forced him to ask himself some hard questions: Why *was* he pushing for marriage? Why was he trying to convince Maggie to move to Rust Creek Falls? How long did he really think an LA transplant would last in a small Montana town? Didn't he learn anything from his painful experience with his ex?

He'd met Shaelyn Everton when he was a student at Montana State University. She didn't really have a major— she was just taking some courses that interested her while she tried to figure out what she wanted to do with her life. Their paths had crossed at a pub on campus—his friend had been hitting on her friend, leaving the two of them to make conversation with one another.

She'd been pretty and sweet and he'd fallen fast and hard. Some of his friends had warned that she didn't want an education just an "MRS" degree, but he didn't care. All that mattered was that they were going to be together.

He'd proposed to her the day of his graduation, and she'd happily accepted. She'd promised that she was excited to go to Rust Creek Falls with him, to spend time with his family and start to plan their wedding.

She'd visited his hometown with him at Christmastime,

a few months earlier, but they'd been so busy with family and holiday events, she didn't have much time to experience the town. She admitted to him, after only a few days, that she was feeling a little bit of culture shock.

He didn't understand what she meant—having been born and raised in Rust Creek Falls, he was certain the town had all the amenities anyone could need. And anything that wasn't readily available in town—specialty shops and fancy restaurants—was close enough in Kalispell.

Her frustration had come to a head one night when she decided to make Salisbury steak for dinner. Unfortunately, she'd forgotten to buy mushrooms when she'd gone into Kalispell to get groceries. She went to Crawford's, but they only had canned, and she had a complete meltdown. Jesse tried to reassure her, suggesting that she could make the recipe without the mushrooms—he wasn't a huge fan, anyway. But she'd refused, insisting that it wouldn't be the same.

It hadn't seemed like a big deal to him, but it had been the beginning of the end for Shaelyn. She didn't know what to do with herself in Rust Creek Falls. She hated that his work at the ranch kept him busy for so many hours of each day. She wanted to spend time with him, to linger in bed late in the morning and enjoy long, leisurely lunches. Then she expected him to come in early and spend the evening hours entertaining her. After a few weeks, he talked his sister into giving Shaelyn a job at the store, but his fiancée had studied art history at university and was appalled by the idea of working in retail—especially in a small-town general store that sold cookies, canned goods and fishing gear, all under one roof.

He'd tried to make her happy. Though it got to the point where he almost dreaded coming home at the end of the day, he reminded himself that there had been a reason he'd fallen in love and planned to spend his life with her. So he would come in after working all day, shower off the dirt and sweat and take her into Kalispell to dinner or to see a movie. He wanted her to be happy, but trying to keep her happy was exhausting him. In retrospect, he was relieved it had only taken her three weeks to realize she couldn't stay in Rust Creek Falls.

She'd claimed to love him but, in the end, she hadn't loved him enough to really try to make their relationship work. He'd come in from checking fences one day to find her engagement ring on the table with a note.

> Jesse,
> I can't do this anymore. I really thought we would be together forever, but I can't stay in this town one more day. If you ever decide you want more than what you've got here, you know where to find me.
> Love,
> Shaelyn

Three weeks was all she'd lasted before deciding that Rust Creek Falls was too small-town for her. And she'd been from Billings. Billings had a population of 165,000 people—a booming metropolis in comparison to Rust Creek Falls, but an insignificant speck on the map in contrast to the more than three million that lived in Los Angeles.

If Shaelyn had been unhappy in Rust Creek Falls, what made him think that Maggie would feel any differently? Why was he pushing for marriage to another woman who would be completely out of her element in the small Montana town?

Maggie was a successful attorney comfortable with

the fast pace and bright lights of the city. She'd spent a few days in Rust Creek Falls—a few days that were an interlude from her ordinary life. In California she could have any kind of cuisine delivered to her door; food options in Rust Creek Falls were limited to the Ace in the Hole, Wings To Go and Daisy's Donuts. LA had concerts, comedy clubs, live theater and multiplexes; the only place to see a movie in Rust Creek Falls was the high school gymnasium, and only there on Friday or Saturday nights.

Of course, people were already talking about how the opening of Maverick Manor—his brother Nate's new resort—could change the atmosphere in Rust Creek Falls. Not everyone was in favor of those changes, but in Thunder Canyon, the opening of their resort a few years ago had brought about big changes and seriously boosted the local economy. It was hoped that Maverick Manor might do the same thing. There would be new shops and eateries, obviously targeting visitors but also benefitting local residents with the expanded availability of goods and services and the creation of new jobs. But those changes wouldn't happen overnight, and even when they did, would they be enough for Maggie? Could a big-city attorney ever be happy in a small town?

Because no matter how many more shops and restaurants moved into the area, Rust Creek Falls was always going to be a small town, and Jesse suspected that asking Maggie to stay would only be setting himself up for another heartache.

Unless he was careful to ensure that his heart didn't get involved.

Maggie had hoped to postpone the inevitable meeting between her parents and the father of her baby, but as soon as Gavin and Christa learned Jesse was coming to town, they were eager for the introductions. So after dinner, she drove to her parents' Hollywood Hills home, where Christa met them at the door.

After kissing her daughter on the cheek, she offered her hand to their guest. "You must be Jesse."

"Yes, ma'am," he confirmed.

And her mother, who rubbed elbows with judges and politicians and movie stars, almost swooned in response to his boyish country charm.

"Please," she said, "call me Christa."

"It's a pleasure to meet you," he said.

"We're eager to get to know you," she told him.

"Too eager to wait until tomorrow," Maggie noted.

Her mother just smiled. "It's a lovely night, so we're having drinks out on the patio, by the pool."

Jesse followed Maggie through the wide-open French doors that led to the enormous stone deck that spread out to encircle the hot tub and kidney-shaped swimming pool. Flames crackled in the outdoor fireplace, adding warmth and light to the seating area.

Her father had been relaxing on one of the dark wicker sofas with a glass of his favorite scotch in his hand, but he set the glass down and rose to his feet when they stepped out onto the patio.

"Maggie's brought her young man to meet us," Christa said to her husband.

Maggie winced at the *her* more than the *young man*, as the possessive pronoun suggested a relationship that didn't really exist.

"Jesse Crawford," he said, offering his hand to her father.

Gavin accepted, probably squeezing Jesse's hand with more force than was necessary—or even polite. She was confident that Jesse could handle anything her father dished out—she was more worried that her baby's father and her own father might find common ground in their belief that an expectant mother should have a husband.

"Can I get you something to drink?" Gavin asked Jesse. "Whiskey? Wine? Beer?"

"I'll have whatever you're having," Jesse said.

"Maggie?"

"I'll just have a glass of water."

Her father dispensed the drinks, then resumed his seat beside his wife. He asked Jesse about his education and his employment, his family and friends, and life in Rust Creek Falls. The questioning wasn't dissimilar to what she'd been put through by Jesse's parents, although she liked to think hers were a little more subtle.

Jesse answered the questions with more patience than Maggie had. When her father paused to sip his drink, she finally asked, "Is the interrogation part of the evening finished yet?"

"I'm just making conversation," Gavin told her.

"Really? Because you've served me steaks that haven't been so thoroughly grilled."

"Maggie," Christa chastised.

But her husband chuckled.

"She's always been quick to defend," he told Jesse. "But if the baby she's carrying turns out to be a girl, she'll undoubtedly be asking the same questions someday."

"Or I will," Jesse said.

Gavin nodded. "Or you will."

"Don't forget you've got a seven-fifteen tee time with the governor's son-in-law in the morning," Christa said to her husband when he got up to refill his drink.

"*If* it doesn't rain," he clarified.

"There's no rain in the forecast," his wife assured him.

"But every time I think there's no rain in the forecast, we get rained out."

"What are you two up to tomorrow?" Christa asked, turning back to her daughter.

"I'm going to show Jesse some of the local sights," Maggie responded. "And since we plan to get an early start, we should head out."

"I know you don't have a spare bedroom in your condo, but you've got a pullout sofa," her father said pointedly.

"Gavin," his wife chided.

He ignored her gentle admonishment. "She might be twenty-eight years old and on her way to becoming a mother herself, but she's still my baby girl," he said.

"Maybe I should move to Montana," Maggie muttered under her breath.

"If only you really meant that," Jesse said, not under his breath at all.

There was a lot to see and do in Los Angeles, and Maggie was happy to play tour guide for Jesse. She took him to Venice Beach, where they skated along the bike path, browsed the shops along the boardwalk, admired the public art walls, detoured around a filming crew and had lunch at a vegetarian café—but only after he made her promise she would never tell any of his friends or family in Montana. He seemed to enjoy spending the time with her, just talking and laughing and getting to know one another. And when they finally got back to her condo at the end of the day, she was sorry to realize the weekend was more than half over.

Less than twenty-four hours after that, she took him back to the airport again. She was glad that he'd come to Los Angeles, that he'd made the effort to see her. Except that she knew it had been an effort, that maintaining a relationship—or trying to establish one—over such a long distance wasn't easy.

And despite the time they'd spent together during the days—and their lovemaking in the nights—they hadn't resolved anything with respect to the baby or their future, and she was afraid they wouldn't anytime soon.

"We're not going to be able to do this every weekend, are we?" he asked when she walked him through the airport to the security checkpoint.

His question confirmed that his thoughts had been following the same path as her own. "Probably not," she admitted.

"When do you think you'll be able to get back to Rust Creek Falls?"

"I don't know. I've got a lot of stuff going on at work this week—" and she hadn't told him the half of it "—but I'll figure something out."

"I wish I had more to offer you."

"What do you mean?"

"My life in Montana is a lot more modest than everything you've got here."

She lifted a shoulder. "Believe me, the shine of Tinseltown wears off after a while."

And as much as she'd enjoyed this weekend in the city with Jesse, she couldn't deny there was a part of her that wished she was going back to Montana with him.

She was still feeling restless and unsettled when she went into work Monday morning. She'd always loved being part of the well-oiled machine that was Alliston & Blake and had thrived in the busy environment. But after her conversation with Brian Nash on Friday, she realized that it really was a machine—and she was just one of hundreds of gears—interchangeable and replaceable.

By early afternoon, she'd reviewed a restructuring proposal, drafted a motion for an injunction and written her letter of resignation—although she hadn't yet decided what, if anything, she was going to do with it.

Needing to stretch her legs, she went into the staff room to get a drink of water.

On her way, she crossed paths with Perry Edler as he was leaving Brian Nash's office.

"Mr. Edler," she said, offering her hand to the man she'd worked with on numerous occasions in the past.

He shook it automatically.

"I'm sorry I wasn't available to meet with you Friday night."

His expression was polite but blank, as if he wasn't entirely sure who she was or why he might have been meeting with her.

"I trust that Amanda was able to respond to any concerns you might have had about your new venture." She was well aware that it was Patricia and not Amanda who had attended the meeting, but she wondered if the COO of Edler Industries was aware.

"Yes," the older man assured her. "Amanda was most helpful."

Which confirmed Maggie's suspicion that he had never asked for her by name, that the associates at Alliston & Blake were all one and the same to the clients. So long as the work was done, they didn't care who did it. And that was okay—the head of an international company was obviously more concerned with the answers to his questions than the identity of the person answering them.

"But maybe you'll be at the next meeting," he said solicitously, because the head of an international company understood that it was easier to stay on top when you had people below to keep you there.

"Maybe I will," she said, but she didn't think it was likely.

She knew that her work mattered, but she was only beginning to realize that she wanted more than that—she wanted to matter. And she would never be anything more than one of those interchangeable gears if she stayed at Alliston & Blake.

She went back to her office and printed her resignation letter.

Chapter Eight

Maggie wasn't usually an impulsive person, but less than twenty-four hours after her brief conversation with Perry Edler, she was back in Rust Creek Falls to meet with Ben Dalton.

"We do a little bit of everything here," the attorney said, in response to her question about his areas of practice. "Although most of it is wills, real estate transactions, the occasional divorce, traffic offenses, minor criminal stuff. What did you do in LA?"

"Mostly corporate law for the past few years, with a focus on mergers and acquisitions," she admitted. "I've already looked into taking the Montana Bar, and I know it's only offered twice a year—in Helena in February or Missoula in July. I was hoping to write in February, but I missed the registration deadline."

"If you think you can be ready to write in February, I might be able to get your name on the list."

"I think I'd do better writing it in February," she admitted. "Because I'm expecting a baby in April."

"Are you planning to get married before then?"

The unexpected question made her pause, because she couldn't imagine any interviewer in LA ever daring to ask any such thing.

"It's a possibility," she told him.

"Because folks around here are pretty conservative,"

Ben warned. "And likely to be suspicious enough of a big-city attorney setting up practice in their backyard. But if you were married to a local boy—assuming the baby's father is a local boy—that would go a long way with the people in this town."

And she knew that if he did offer her a position, she'd have to remember that things were done a little bit differently here. With that thought in mind, she nodded. "One of the reasons I wanted to move to Rust Creek Falls was to be closer to the baby's father, so that we can share the parenting."

"A smart decision," Ben told her. "My wife chose to be a stay-at-home mother, and I'm grateful our six kids had the benefit of having her around full-time, but she'll be the first to admit that every aspect of parenting is made easier by sharing it with someone."

He talked about his wife with an easy affection that spoke of their thirty-seven years and the experience of raising half a dozen kids together. He had a copy of their wedding picture in a gold frame on his desk and told Maggie it was a lucky man who could, after almost four decades, honestly say he loved his wife even more now than the day he married her.

Rust Creek Falls might have been a small town, but there were still a lot of people that Maggie had yet to meet and a lot of familial connections she hadn't begun to make. For example, it wasn't until Ben pulled out his cell phone to show off the latest snapshots of his brand-new grandson that she learned his daughter Paige was married to Sutter Traub, the owner of Traub Stables—Jesse's boss. They'd recently had a baby boy—Carter Benjamin Traub—and the proud grandpa had more than a hundred photos of the little guy on his cell phone.

The baby was adorable, and just looking at the pictures

made Maggie long for the day when her baby would finally be in her arms. Except when she remembered her first interaction with Jesse's ten-month-old-niece—then her anticipation was tempered by a healthy dose of apprehension.

"He offered me a job," Maggie told Lissa, when she got back to her cousin's house after the interview.

"Of course he did," Lissa said smugly. "He's never going to find a more qualified candidate than you to add to his practice."

"I'm not qualified yet," she reminded her cousin. "I still have to pass the Montana Bar."

Lissa waved a hand dismissively. "I'm more interested in the details about your wedding, such as what your matron of honor will be wearing."

Maggie shook her head. "The only thing I accepted today was a job, not a marriage proposal."

"But you *are* going to marry Jesse, aren't you?"

"I don't know," she admitted.

"So let me see if I'm following this," Lissa said. "You felt an instant connection to Jesse and fell into bed together. It was the best sex of your life and you hoped it was the start of a real relationship, then you found out you were having his baby and he proposed, but you don't know if you should marry him?"

Maggie nodded. "That about sums it up."

"I need a little help with the 'why' part," her cousin admitted.

"Why what?"

"Why you don't want to marry him."

"Because I love him."

Lissa took her hands. "Sweetie, you're not just my cousin but one of my best friends in the world, but I have to admit that right now, I have serious concerns about your sanity."

Maggie managed a smile even as her eyes filled with tears. "I want him to love me, too."

"You don't think he does?"

"I know he doesn't." And she told Lissa what Jesse had said about common goals being more important to the success of a marriage than love.

"Clearly Jesse Crawford is an idiot. But," Lissa continued, when Maggie opened her mouth to protest, "since he's the idiot you love, we're going to have to come up with a plan."

"A plan?"

"To make sure he falls in love with you, too."

"I don't think that's something you can plan," Maggie said.

Her cousin smiled. "A smart woman has a plan for everything."

Gage and Lissa decided to go into Kalispell for dinner. They invited Maggie to go with them, but she declined. She needed some time to think about her future—and she needed to call Jesse. Before she had a chance to do so, there was a knock on the door, and when she opened it, he was there.

"Jesse—hi." Her instinctive pleasure at seeing him was mixed with guilt as she realized that she hadn't told him about her plans to come to Rust Creek Falls this week. "I guess news travels fast in a small town."

He nodded. "Of course, I didn't believe it when Nina told me she overheard Lani Dalton tell Melba Strickland that her father was interviewing 'that city lawyer.' But then Will Baker told me that he saw you and Ben having lunch at the Ace in the Hole."

"Who needs Twitter when you've got the Rust Creek Falls grapevine?"

"Why are you here?" Jesse asked. "I thought you had some big project to work on with your boss at Alliston & Blake."

She stepped away from the door so that he could enter. "Why don't you come in so we can talk about it?"

He followed her into the kitchen, hanging his jacket over the back of a chair before settling into it.

"Do you want anything to drink?"

He shook his head. "No, I'm fine, thanks."

She turned on the kettle to make herself a cup of peppermint tea, more because she wanted something to do than because she wanted the tea.

"I handed in my resignation at Alliston & Blake yesterday."

He opened his mouth, closed it again, as if he wasn't quite sure what to say, how to respond to her news. "Okay—I'll admit I didn't see that one coming."

She shrugged. "It was time. Maybe past time. Technically, I'm supposed to give two weeks' notice, but since I haven't used all of my vacation this year—actually, I haven't used all of it in any of the past few years—I'm officially on vacation right now."

"And your lunch with Ben today?" he prompted.

"He offered me a job." She didn't tell him that she'd accepted, because she didn't want him to immediately rush to the same conclusion that Lissa had done.

"You're thinking about moving to Rust Creek Falls?"

She nodded. "I'm not sure of any of the other details yet, but I'm sure that I want you to be part of our baby's life." She poured the boiling water over the tea bag inside her cup, then carried it to the table and sat down across from him. "You went away to school, right?"

"Montana State University in Bozeman."

"When you graduated, did you ever think about exploring options anywhere else?"

He shook his head. "Nowhere else is home."

She couldn't help but smile at his conviction. "It must be nice, to know without a doubt that you are exactly where you belong."

"You don't feel like that in LA?"

"I wouldn't be making this move if I did," she told him.

"Are you going to marry me?"

She hesitated. "I still think marriage is a little extreme."

"And yet people have been doing it for thousands of years."

She smiled. "Yes, and since it's the twenty-first century, our child is unlikely to be ostracized by society if his or her parents aren't married."

"Archaic attitudes are still pervasive in society," he said, in an echo of Ben's comments earlier that day.

"And more so in Montana than California," she acknowledged.

"Undoubtedly," he agreed.

"Despite that, there are aspects of this town that really appeal to me, too."

"Such as?"

"The teacher-to-student ratio in the schools. It's widely theorized that students in smaller classes learn better. The public high school I went to had two thousand students. The secondary school here has a population that isn't even one-tenth of that."

"And only one teacher."

She laughed, because she was almost 100 percent certain he was joking. "And I like the sense of community," she said. "Everywhere you go, you cross paths with someone you know."

"I don't always consider that a plus," he admitted.

"It is," she insisted. "You might not always agree with your friends and neighbors, but you know you can count on them.

"Lissa told me what it was like, after the floods last year. How the residents rallied to help one another. Even the Crawfords and the Traubs worked together."

"That's true."

"You don't see a lot of that in LA. I'm not saying that neighbors don't ever help neighbors, but it's not the usual mindset. It's a town built on glitz and glamour and climbing over other people to get to the top."

"Why would you ever want to leave such a place?"

She smiled at his dry tone. "I also like the idea of a job with more regular hours, so that I'd have more time to spend with my baby."

"And your husband."

She shook her head. "You're like a wave crashing against a rock, determined to erode my resistance."

"Is it working?"

"It might be," she acknowledged. "And if I did decide to marry you, then what would you do?"

"Call the preacher to book a date for the wedding before you changed your mind," he replied without hesitation.

"The wedding is the easy part—it's the marriage I'm worried about."

"I'm not going to tell you that you shouldn't worry," he said. "Because I think you're right—if we want our marriage to succeed, we're both going to have to work at it. But the fact that you're having my baby means that we both have a vested interest in its success, and I'm willing to do whatever it takes to give our child the happy and stable family that he—or she—deserves."

"Then I guess, since it seems we both want the same thing, you should call the preacher."

"Really?"

She nodded.

He whooped and lifted her off her feet, spinning her around. And the sheer joy of being in his arms and sharing his joy convinced Maggie that she'd made the right decision.

She still had some concerns—aside from agreeing to marry a man who didn't love her, there was the uncertainty about whether or not she would be able to make the transition to life in the country. But if Lissa could do it—if her cousin could make the change from Manhattan to Montana—then Maggie was confident she could adjust, too.

But Lissa had worked her butt off to prove herself to the people of Rust Creek Falls after the flood the previous year. On behalf of Bootstraps, a New York–based charitable organization, she'd rallied volunteers, coordinated their schedules and duties, and essentially gone door-to-door assisting families in need and helping repair damage. Along the way she'd fallen in love with the highly respected sheriff, which had helped the townspeople fall in love with her. Even so, Gage's mother had expressed concern when her son had got involved with Lissa. Apparently the local residents had some pretty strong opinions about "city people" and not necessarily good ones.

And then Maggie had swept into town from Los Angeles, and what had she done? She'd helped get Arthur Swinton out of jail—and while his illegal activities had targeted the residents of Thunder Canyon, the people of Rust Creek Falls weren't unaware of what he'd done. As if representing the convict wasn't bad enough, she'd seduced Jesse Crawford and got pregnant in order to trap him into marriage.

Of course, that wasn't at all how things had really happened, but she didn't doubt that at least some of the locals would view the situation in exactly that way.

"At the risk of you changing your mind before I've even put a ring on your finger, I have to ask—do you think you'll miss the hustle and bustle of LA?"

"It's not as if I'm never going back there," she pointed out. "I do still have family in California."

"How are they going to feel about you moving so far away?"

"My parents have always encouraged me to follow my own path."

"Even if that path leads you to a small town in the middle of nowhere?"

"Are you trying to convince me to stay or go?"

"I just want to be sure you know what you're getting into," he told her. "I couldn't imagine living anywhere else, but I know the open space and isolation aren't for everyone. Winters, in particular, can be harsh, especially for someone who is accustomed to having all the amenities of the big city within walking distance."

"So who was she?"

"Who was who?"

"The girlfriend from the big city who did a number on you," she clarified.

He didn't say anything.

"Don't make me go into town searching for tidbits of gossip," she teased.

It wasn't a sincere threat, of course, but Jesse finally answered.

"Her name was Shaelyn," he said. "And for all of three weeks, she was my fiancée."

"Oh." And how silly was it that Maggie was disappointed to realize she wasn't the first woman he'd ever proposed to. "How many times have you been engaged?"

"Just two."

"Was she pregnant?"

He shook his head.

"So you proposed to her because you loved her," she realized.

"I thought I did," he admitted.

But Maggie knew it had been more than a thought to have scarred him so deeply.

He'd told her he didn't want to fall in love—but that was only because he'd already been there, done that. And while her heart was filled to overflowing with feelings for him, his heart was still in pieces, broken by another woman.

Not exactly the auspicious start she'd envisioned for their life together.

True to his word, Jesse called the preacher that same night, and their wedding was scheduled for Saturday afternoon—only four days away.

Christa, Gavin and Ryan all had to do some serious rearranging of their schedules, but they managed to fly into Montana on Friday. Shane and his wife, Gianna, drove up from Thunder Canyon on the same day, and the Roarkes had an impromptu family reunion at Strickland's Boarding House, where they were all staying.

On Wednesday, Lissa had taken Maggie into Kalispell to go shopping. Maggie didn't want to buy her wedding dress without her mother's approval, so every dress that she tried on, Lissa took a picture and emailed it to Christa, who would email back her thoughts and suggestions.

After the fourth picture, Lissa's cell phone rang. Christa was crying happy tears on the other end of the line because she knew that dress was "the one," and she gave her credit card information to the clerk over the phone to ensure that Maggie walked out of the store with it in hand.

And on the day of the wedding, as she helped her daughter into the gown, Christa's eyes misted over again. "Look at you," she said softly, almost reverently.

Maggie did so, smiling as she took in her reflection in the full-length mirror. "I look like a bride," she said, turning to show off the dress from all sides.

It was a strapless design with a sweetheart neckline, a bodice covered in sparkly beads that hugged her breasts, and a full skirt that skimmed the floor.

"The most beautiful bride I've ever seen," her mother said, brushing moisture from her cheeks.

"I'm sure Dad would have something to say about that," Maggie countered. Then she lifted up the hem of her skirt to show her the cowboy boots on her feet. "What do you think? Lissa says she's going to make a cowgirl out of me yet."

"I think, if Lissa says so, I wouldn't bet against it."

Maggie smiled again. "I can't believe it's my wedding day already."

"It seems like only yesterday that you called to tell us you'd accepted Jesse's proposal," her mother said.

"You mean instead of actually being four days ago?"

Christa fussed with the headpiece. "I've never heard of anyone putting together a wedding in four days."

"That's because no one else had Lissa taking care of all the details."

"Probably true," her mother agreed.

Maggie turned to take her hands. "Are you disappointed that we wanted to get married here?"

"It's *your* wedding," her mother said. "And I can understand why you'd want to take your vows where you're going to start your life with your new husband. If I'm disappointed about anything, it's only that we didn't have enough time to plan a proper wedding."

"So you think this is going to be an improper wedding?"

The gentle teasing made Christa smile, even through her tears. "You always did know how to twist words to make your point. It's one of the reasons you're such a good attorney."

"I learned from the best," she said.

"Hopefully I also taught you that there's more to life than the law."

"That's why I left my job at Alliston & Blake."

"I only wished you'd left there sooner," her mother admitted. "They demanded far too much of you and gave you very little in return. If you'd come to work at Roarke & Associates—"

"I would have always wondered if I earned my position or got it on the basis of my name."

Christa sighed. "As much as it frustrates me to know that you believed it, I can understand."

"You'll get to meet my new boss and his wife at the wedding."

"I'm looking forward to it," her mother said.

"Knock, knock," Lissa said, pushing open the door. "Mabel sent me up to let you know that the photographer's here."

"Then I'll go get the father of the bride and meet you both downstairs in ten minutes."

Since Jesse had to pick up his tux in Kalispell the day of the wedding, he decided to take it directly to the church and get ready there.

So much had happened since the day Maggie told him she was pregnant, it was hard to believe that only two weeks had passed. He'd known right away that he wanted to marry her and be a father to their child, and his conviction had not wavered. But as the clock ticked closer and closer to four o'clock and their scheduled wedding, he found himself worrying more and more that Maggie might be having second thoughts.

He suspected Shaelyn's most recent phone call was responsible for some of his concern. Although he hadn't spoken to his former fiancée, there had been a message on his machine when he got home the night that Maggie had finally agreed to marry him. Shaelyn had asked him to call her back, but of course he hadn't. She was his past and he was determined to focus on his future with Maggie.

He should feel jubilant—Maggie was going to make her life with him and their child in Rust Creek Falls. He was getting everything he wanted. But what was she getting? She was moving away from her family, her friends, giving up a career. Yes, she was planning to write the State Bar exam in the new year, and he had no doubt that she would soon be licensed to practice in Montana, but he also knew that she wouldn't have the same kind of career here that she could have if she stayed in LA.

Which was one of the reasons she'd agreed to do this—to give her life balance, so that she could be a mother *and* an attorney. But it seemed to him that she was giving up more than she was getting in return, and he couldn't help but wonder if she might come to resent him because of the changes she'd felt compelled to make to her life.

But if there was another—a better—way to work things out, he couldn't see it. He didn't want to live more than twelve hundred miles away from his child. And he didn't want his child raised by someone else while Maggie worked sixty hours a week to pay for that care.

A knock on the door jolted him out of his reverie. Assuming it was Nate, his best man, he invited him to come in.

But when the door opened, it wasn't his oldest brother who walked through it—it was his former fiancée.

Chapter Nine

"Shaelyn."

Jesse stared at her for a long moment, not knowing what else to say. He couldn't believe she was here, and he couldn't begin to fathom why.

"Hello, Jesse." She smiled at him—the same slow, seductive smile that used to be the prelude to all kinds of things.

She looked good—but then, Shaelyn always did. She had the fragile beauty of a china doll: silky hair, porcelain skin, delicate features. She was the type of woman that a man instinctively wanted to cherish and protect, as he'd once vowed to do.

But looking at her now, he felt nothing more than surprise—and maybe some apprehension. He hadn't seen her in seven years and couldn't understand why she'd shown up after so long—and on his wedding day, no less. "What are you doing here?"

"I saw your mother and your sisters in Missoula," his former fiancée explained. "Natalie told me that they were shopping for dresses for your wedding."

"Why were you in Missoula?"

"I've been working at the university for the past four years—at the Museum of Art & Culture."

"I thought you were in Helena. Isn't your husband some kind of advisor to the governor?"

"Ex-husband," she said with a small smile. "I moved to Missoula after the divorce, almost three years ago."

"Oh." He wasn't quite sure what else he was supposed to say. "I'm sorry it didn't work out?"

She offered a weak smile. "I should have realized our marriage was doomed from the start—because I never stopped loving you."

She waited a beat, but Jesse remained silent.

"I was hoping you would say that you feel the same way."

"I don't," he said bluntly.

"I know it's been a long time—"

"Speaking of time, I really don't have time for this right now."

"If we don't do this now, it's going to be too late."

"It's already too late."

She shook her head. "You told me that you loved me."

"Because I did," he confirmed. *"Seven years ago."*

"And now?"

"Now I'm marrying someone else."

She lifted her chin, her gaze challenging. "Do you love her?"

"Why else would I be marrying her?"

"That's what I'm trying to figure out," she said.

"We've been apart longer than we were together," he pointed out. "And I promise—I'm *not* still in love with you."

As he said those words, he realized—without a doubt—that they were true. He was completely over Shaelyn. Yes, he'd loved her once, but that was in the past. He'd been young and infatuated, wanting to be with the woman who claimed she wanted to be with him. When she'd gone, he'd realized that he hadn't missed Shaelyn so much as he'd missed being with someone.

"But you still haven't said that you're in love with her."

"I'm in love with Maggie," he said, because it seemed that speaking the words was the only way to get his former fiancée out of the way so he could marry the mother of his child.

"Okay, then—" she took a step back "—I guess I should offer my congratulations."

"Thank you, Shaelyn."

But, of course, she couldn't leave it at that. "I hope she loves you, too, Jesse. Enough to trade in the glitz and glamour of Hollywood for the tedium and simplicity of Big Sky Country."

And with those words, she tossed her hair over her shoulder and stalked out, passing the groom's best man on the way.

"What the hell was *she* doing here?" Nate wanted to know.

"I'm not entirely sure," Jesse admitted.

His family had never taken to Shaelyn, despite the fact that he'd planned to marry her. Nate, specifically, had expressed disapproval of her apparent lack of ambition to do anything other than get married.

"What did she say to put that look on your face?"

Jesse just shook his head.

"Don't let her mess with your mind," Nate warned.

"She didn't say anything that I haven't already heard a thousand times."

Except for the fact that she was still in love with him, and he wasn't going to get into that with his brother. Because, as he'd said to Maggie when he first proposed to her, he wasn't looking for love.

So why was he bothered by Shaelyn's suggestion that Maggie might not love him enough?

* * *

As his wife fussed with his tie, determined to get it just right before he walked their daughter down the aisle, Gavin stared stonily ahead, trying *not* to think about the reason he was in this tux.

"You're the father of the bride—try to look happy."

"Even if I'm not?"

Christa sighed. "You should be happy for your daughter—this is what she wants."

"She's only twenty-eight years old and she's been so busy building a career, she's barely dated. How can she know what she wants?" he demanded.

"No one knows her mind like our Maggie," his wife assured him. "A fact that you've been lamenting since she was a toddler."

He smiled, because it was true, but the smile quickly faded. "You don't think he coerced her into this marriage because she's pregnant?"

"I think she wouldn't let herself be coerced if she didn't want to be."

He continued to scowl. "She's our baby girl."

"Our baby girl's going to have a baby of her own in a few months," Christa reminded him gently.

"And she's going to have that baby more than a thousand miles away from us."

"I know you think Montana is the middle of nowhere, but we managed to get here today, didn't we?"

"You think I'm being ridiculous," he realized.

"I think you're being a father." She tugged on his tie, bringing his mouth down to hers for a quick kiss. "And a very handsome father of the bride you are."

"The mother of the bride looks pretty good, too."

She arched a brow. "Pretty good?"

He grinned and slipped his arm around her waist. "I love you, Christa."

"I love you, too."

"I just hope that, forty years from now, Maggie and Jesse will be as happy as we are."

"No one can know what the future holds," she told her husband, "but I have no doubt that when you walk our daughter down the aisle today, she will be marrying the man she loves."

The groom's parents, already seated in the church, weren't any more enthusiastic about the forthcoming nuptials than the bride's father.

"I hope he isn't making a mistake," Todd Crawford said, drumming his fingers on his knee.

His wife clasped her hands together in her lap. "What else could he do, under the circumstances?"

"Nothing," her husband admitted. "A man needs to take responsibility for his actions, and a child needs a father."

"Then why are you griping?"

"I just wish, if he had to knock up someone, he'd chosen a local girl who might actually stay put in this town."

"Except that one or more of his brothers has dated most of the single women in Rust Creek Falls," she pointed out drily.

"There are plenty of women in Kalispell or even other parts of Montana."

"Like Billings?"

He winced at the mention of the hometown of the groom's former fiancée. "Okay, so that didn't work out so well for him. But I'm not sure this is going to be any better. She's from Los Angeles for Christ's sake."

"Don't swear," his wife admonished.

"She's not going to be happy here."

"You don't know that—look at her cousin, Lissa. She came from New York and yet she settled in with the sheriff with no difficulty."

As was usual when Todd couldn't refute an argument, he said nothing. But his jaw remained stubbornly set.

"This all started when he went to work at Traub Stables," he said, after another minute had passed.

Laura frowned. "What?"

"It's those damn Traubs—they lured Jesse away from home, from his roots."

His wife sighed. "You know Jesse's heart has always been with the horses."

Todd shook his head. "As if it wasn't bad enough that everyone in town knows that our son is working for a Traub, now he's marrying a California girl."

"Could you try to focus on something else—at least for today?"

"Like what?"

"Like the fact that we're going to be grandparents again."

"That's if she sticks around long enough for us to meet the baby," her husband grumbled.

Maggie had lived her whole life in Los Angeles, where there was no shortage of handsome men. She worked in a law firm where men lived in suits. But she was certain she'd never seen anyone as handsome as Jesse Crawford. And she knew none of those other men had ever affected her the way he did. Never had any one of those men made her breath catch in her throat or her heart pound so hard and fast against her ribs she was certain everyone must be able to hear it.

But when she took her first steps down the aisle and saw Jesse standing at the altar, that's exactly what happened.

She didn't even remember the exchange of vows; the words were somehow lost in the excitement of the realization that she was going to be Mrs. Jesse Crawford. She did remember the kiss. Although it was chaste in comparison to other kisses they'd shared, there was heat in the brief touch of his mouth to hers, enough to heighten her awareness and anticipation.

Now she was in his arms again, sharing their first dance as husband and wife.

As she turned around the floor, she caught a glimpse of her parents—Christa dabbing her eyes with Gavin's handkerchief—and Jesse's parents—Laura's smile obviously forced, Todd's attention on the drink in his hand.

"I think your mother disapproves of the fact that I'm wearing a white dress," Maggie said.

Jesse looked down at his bride—the most beautiful woman he'd ever known, looking even more beautiful than ever. "You don't need to worry about my mother's—or anyone else's—approval."

At nineteen weeks, Maggie wasn't obviously pregnant. It was only because he'd been intimate with her slender body that Jesse was aware of the subtle bump that was proof of their baby growing inside of her.

"I'm not really. But I know people are already speculating about the reasons for our getting married so quickly."

"People are always going to talk about something."

"I know," she admitted. "Although it's a little unnerving to realize that the Hollywood paparazzi has nothing on the Rust Creek Falls grapevine."

"You're a celebrity here," he told her.

"The city slicker who shamelessly seduced the quiet cowboy and trapped him into marriage?"

He tipped her chin up, forcing her to meet his gaze.

"I don't feel trapped," he promised her. "I feel incredibly lucky."

Then he brushed his lips against hers.

And the way she kissed him back gave him hope that, before the night was out, he'd get even luckier.

After the cake-cutting ceremony, Maggie slipped away to use the ladies' room. Lissa had been taking her duties as matron of honor seriously and had barely left the bride's side, but she was dancing with her husband now and Maggie didn't want to interrupt.

It was a bit tricky to maneuver her skirts in the narrow stall, but she managed and was just about to flush when she heard the *click-clack* of heels on tile. Several pairs, by the sound of it, accompanied by talking and laughter.

The words she heard made her pause with her fingers on the handle.

"Guess who stopped by to see the groom before the wedding," an unfamiliar female voice said.

"Who?" a second woman wanted to know.

"Shaelyn Everton."

"Who?" the second speaker asked again.

"Jesse's ex," yet another voice responded, sounding impatient. "The one he was engaged to for all of three weeks."

Inside her bathroom stall, Maggie sucked in a breath. Thankfully, the other women were too focused on their conversation to hear her.

"How do you know this?"

"Brad told me that Nate caught them together in the anteroom before the ceremony."

"Caught them doing what?" There was more glee than curiosity in the tone, suggesting that the second woman enjoyed a juicy scandal.

Maggie pressed a hand to her stomach, desperate to still its sudden churning.

Her friend laughed. "Nothing like that," she chided. "They were just talking."

"Oh." Woman Number Two didn't hide her disappointment while the bride exhaled a long, slow breath. "What was she doing here?"

"Trying to make a final play for Jesse would be my guess."

"Because breaking his heart once wasn't enough?"

"She messed him up, that's for sure," the first woman commented. "I remember hearing his mom tell my mom that she didn't think he'd ever get over her."

"That was a long time ago," someone else said. "And he seems happy with Maggie."

"For now," the first speaker allowed.

"Give her a chance," the third woman suggested.

"Kristin's just mad that Maggie got him into bed and she never did."

"I've always liked the strong, silent type," the first speaker, now identified as Kristin, admitted. "But Brad is every bit as cute as his brother—maybe even more."

"But why was Shaelyn here?" The second woman finally circled back to the original topic of conversation. "I thought she married some other guy."

"She did, but they're divorced now. And while she might have been the one to leave Jesse, the rumor is that she never got over him."

The women had apparently finished their primping and started toward the exit, as evidenced by the *click-clack* on the tiles and their fading voices. "I don't think he…"

Maggie stayed in the bathroom stall until she was sure they were gone, and then for a few minutes more to compose herself.

She didn't know what to make of that entire exchange. What she did know was that, even if Shaelyn still wanted Jesse, she wasn't going to get him.

Because the shy, sexy cowboy was Maggie's husband now.

Jesse warily eyed the beer that Maggie's oldest brother offered to him. "Is it poisoned?"

Shane Roarke grinned. "You haven't given me any reason to want to make my sister a widow...yet."

"Then I'll make sure I don't," he said, accepting the bottle.

"I wish I could be sure that Maggie will be happy here."

"You don't think she will be?"

"Let's just say I have my doubts." Shane sipped his own beer.

"Wasn't it just a couple of years ago that you decided to make your home in Montana?"

"Yeah, but I moved around a lot before then," his new brother-in-law pointed out. "Maggie, on the other hand, has been working her tail off for the past five years to establish herself at Alliston & Blake."

"From my perspective, she worked too long and too hard for too little."

"I don't disagree—but it was her choice."

"So was this," Jesse assured him.

"That's what I have to wonder about," Shane said. "Because this whole situation—quitting her job, moving twelve hundred miles away, having a whirlwind wedding—isn't Maggie. She doesn't rush into anything."

She hadn't dragged her feet at all the day they met, but that was hardly something that would gain him points with her brother.

"She walked down that aisle of her own free will."

"It looked that way," Shane agreed. "But one of the women I work with just had a baby, and I have to tell you— pregnant women have all those hormones to deal with that mess with their heads and their hearts.

"I'm not sure Maggie knows what she wants right now, but you managed to convince her that you should be together for the sake of your baby. She's smart, but she's probably scared, too. The prospect of having a baby on her own had to be a little daunting, especially when her pregnancy ended any hopes of ever getting a partnership at Alliston & Blake."

He must have noticed Jesse's scowl, because he swore softly. "I guess she didn't tell you about that."

"No, she didn't."

"I think she was planning to leave, anyway," Shane said now. "But when her boss found out she was pregnant, it expedited the process."

"So you think she married me because she was in danger of losing her job?"

"No. She wouldn't have had any trouble getting another job in LA—and not just at our parents' firm. But I think marrying you gave her the excuse she needed to make a big change.

"I'm just not sure, because everything happened so fast, that she's not going to regret it in a month or two and realize she isn't cut out for life in Small Town, Montana."

Jesse thought about what Shane had said for a long time after the other man had gone.

There was no doubt he'd pushed Maggie to the altar because it was what he wanted for their baby. She'd voiced some objections, and he'd disregarded each and every one. Even her concerns about her clients in LA had been discounted, because they hadn't been as important to him as giving their baby a family. But they'd been important to her...

Damn.

He didn't know if what Shane had said about pregnancy hormones was true—but in case it was, he was going to give her time and space to decide if this was truly what she wanted.

As was usual for a bride, Maggie spent a lot of time dancing with various guests. After the first dance with her new husband, she took a turn around the floor with her father, then Jesse's father, then Ben Dalton. She danced and chatted with each of her new brothers-in-law and several other residents whose names she wasn't even sure she would remember. When her brother Ryan snagged her for a spin, she was grateful that she didn't have to keep up any pretenses—at least for the next three minutes.

"When you decide to make some changes in your life, you do it in a big way," he mused.

"It was time," she said lightly.

"Maybe," he acknowledged. "But this is the twenty-first century—you don't have to get married to have a baby."

"I know," she said, and she loved her brother for his ability to support nontraditional choices.

"You should also know that I'm having a really hard time not kicking that cowboy's ass for doing the things he did with you that resulted in you getting pregnant."

She held back a smile. "You could *try* to kick his ass."

Her brother's eyes narrowed. "You don't think I could take him?"

"I'm a big girl, you know. It's not like I was an innocent virgin seduced by a big bad cowboy. I wanted him every bit as much as he wanted me."

Ryan winced. "I don't need to know things like that."

"Apparently you do."

"I just want you to be happy, and I'm not convinced you will be with him. He's not at all like any of the other guys you've dated."

"No, he's not," she agreed. "And I think it says something that I never fell in love with any of those other guys."

He looked at her carefully. "You really are in love with him?"

"This is the twenty-first century," she said, echoing his words back to him. "I wouldn't be marrying him for any other reason."

"So I can't kick his ass?"

"You can't even try."

"Okay," he relented. "But if he ever makes you unhappy, you let me know."

"I'll let you know," she promised.

"Maybe I should kick Shane's ass," Ryan suggested.

"Why?"

"Because if he hadn't enlisted our help to get Arthur Swinton out of jail, there wouldn't be any Grace Traub Community Center, and you would never have come to Rust Creek Falls and met Jesse Crawford."

"I would have come anyway for Lissa and Gage's wedding," she pointed out to him.

"I guess you would have," he allowed.

"Look on the bright side—now you have twice as many reasons to visit Montana. And maybe you'll find the woman of your dreams in Big Sky Country, too."

"There's only one woman for me—Lady Justice."

"Does she keep you warm at night?"

"No, but there are other women who satisfy those needs."

"I don't need details," Maggie said.

"You weren't going to get any," he assured her.

The song ended, and he stepped back but continued to hold her hands. "I'm going to miss you."

"You're going to miss stealing the Yorkshire pudding from my plate at Sunday-night dinner."

He grinned. "That, too."

Jesse caught up to his bride as she was kissing her younger brother's cheek. Since he'd already done the verbal sparring routine with her older brother, he merely nodded to Ryan and spoke to Maggie.

"Apparently the guests want the bride and groom to share one last dance."

"It's barely ten o'clock," she protested.

"Most of the people here are ranchers who will be up before the sun rises in the morning," he reminded her.

"Then I guess we should have that dance."

He took her hand and led her back to the middle of the floor. His youngest sister, acting as DJ, announced their final dance, and Maggie lifted a brow when she recognized the opening bars of the song.

"Did you request this?" she asked, as they moved in time to the Rolling Stones' "Wild Horses."

He shook his head. "It was Natalie's choice."

But Maggie just smiled, appreciating his sister's off-beat sense of humor. Or maybe she just appreciated that it wasn't a traditional sappy ballad.

"How are you holding up?" he asked her now.

"I'm doing okay."

"It's been a long day."

"It's been a crazy week," she clarified. "I can't believe we managed to put together a wedding in only three days."

"With a little help from our friends and families."

"A *lot* of help."

He nodded his agreement. Shane Roarke, head chef at

the Gallatin Room, the four-star restaurant at the Thunder Canyon Resort, was their connection to the resort's pastry chef, who had agreed to make the wedding cake; Nina had a friend who did the flowers; Lissa, Maggie's matron of honor and the undisputed queen of organization, had supervised the decorating, ensuring that the utilitarian community room was transformed into a winter wonderland, including potted Christmas trees with white lights and silver bows, silver and white streamers, bouquets of helium-filled balloons and white poinsettias in silver pots on the tables.

It was beautiful and festive, but what made the day perfect for Maggie was the identity of her groom.

And she was looking forward to their perfect night that would follow their perfect day.

Chapter Ten

Someone had brought Jesse's truck to the front door of the community hall to expedite the bride and groom's exit from the reception.

Maggie smiled when she saw that the vehicle had been decorated with paper flowers and an enormous heart proclaiming Just Married. Jesse offered his hand to help her into the cab, and when she took it, a definite frisson of electricity passed between them.

Neither of them said much on the drive back to his house. Maggie's mind and heart were so cluttered with emotion and anticipation, she could barely hold on to a thought. But when she looked down at the hands folded in her lap, and at the rings on her finger that confirmed that she was definitely and undeniably Jesse Crawford's wife, she knew—maybe for the first time in her life—that she was exactly where she wanted to be.

It wasn't until he shut off the engine that she realized they'd arrived at his house. Now her home, too. And it was their wedding night. Nerves and excitement tangled in her belly as she reached for the gift bag that Lissa had thrust into her hands as she was leaving the hall.

Jesse came around to her door again and helped her out of the truck. But she'd barely put her feet on the ground when he swept her off them and into his arms.

"What are you doing?"

"It's traditional for the groom to carry his bride over the threshold," he told her.

She knew that, of course. And the fact that he'd insisted they marry before the birth of their child proved he was a traditional guy. But both of those facts were lost in the giddy excitement and sheer pleasure of being carried in strong arms.

He turned the handle and pushed open the door. "Welcome home, Mrs. Crawford."

She smiled at him. "Thank you, Mr. Crawford."

He gently set her onto her feet, only then seeming to notice the silver bag in her hand with the pale pink tissue sticking out of the top. "What's that?"

"A gift. From Lissa."

"I thought Justin loaded all of the presents into his truck to bring over tomorrow."

"All except this one," she confirmed.

Thankfully, he didn't ask any more questions about it. Instead he said, "I'll go get your suitcases."

"Okay."

He disappeared outside again, returning a few minutes later with the two bags of what she'd deemed to be essential clothing items and toiletries. The rest of her belongings were still in LA, but packed up and ready to be shipped. He set them down inside the door to remove his coat and boots, then carried the suitcases up the stairs.

Maggie hovered inside the door, not quite certain what to do. Reminding herself that she wasn't a guest here—although she still felt like one—she sat down on the bench beside the door and removed her wrap and boots.

She'd loved the sleeveless-style dress when she'd tried it on in the bridal shop in Kalispell, but she wished now that someone had warned her that a November bride in Montana should have sleeves. Long sleeves. And a high collar. But then she remembered the way Jesse had looked at her when he first saw her in the dress, how the heat in his eyes had warmed every inch of her body from her head to her toes.

She moved toward the stone fireplace and imagined flames crackling and flickering as they'd been the first day she'd been here—was it really only two weeks earlier? So much had happened since the day that she'd told Jesse about their baby, it was hard to believe such a short span of time had passed.

She wondered if Jesse would build a fire tonight. She had a fantasy—perhaps born of reading too many romance novels—of making love by a fire, and the thick sheepskin in front of the hearth only fueled that fantasy.

She curled her toes into the fluffy rug as the scene played out in great detail in her mind. He would move slowly toward her, his eyes—filled with unbridled heat and wicked promises—locked on hers. Then he would take her hands in his, drawing her down to the carpet, so they were kneeling and facing one another. Then he would slowly peel away her clothes as he kissed her, his lips moving from her mouth to her throat to her breasts—

"Maggie?"

She gasped, as his voice jolted her out of her fantasy. "I didn't hear you come back down the stairs," she admitted.

"Are you okay?"

"Fine," she said quickly. "I was just thinking a fire might help take the chill out of the air."

"It's kind of late," he told her. "If I started one now, I wouldn't be able to go to bed until it was completely out."

"I didn't think about that," she admitted, trying not to feel disappointed that his response had been more practical than romantic. Besides, he'd carried her over the threshold, which was an undeniably romantic gesture. Not quite as romantic as carrying her directly upstairs and to his bed, but romantic nonetheless.

"Did you want anything?" Jesse asked. "A cup of tea or a glass of water?"

She shook her head. "I think I'll just go get ready for bed."

"Okay."

"Can I just get your help with something?" She turned around, showing him her back. "There's a little hook at the top of the zipper that I can't reach."

"Oh. Um. Sure."

She felt the brush of his knuckles against her bare skin as he wrestled with the tiny closure, and goose bumps danced up her spine. The catch released and he lifted his hands away.

"And the zipper," she prompted. "If you could just lower it a couple of inches."

The soft rasp of the pull tracking along the twin rows of tiny teeth—the only sound in the quiet room—was tantalizingly seductive. As the zipper inched downward, the fabric of her bodice parted, exposing a V of skin between her shoulder blades. The air was cool, but she felt hot all over. Hot and achy and needy.

"How's that?" His voice was low, husky, and she knew he was as aroused as she was.

Maybe he didn't love her, but he wanted her, and that would be enough for now.

"That's great—thanks."

She picked up the gift bag again and carried it upstairs to the bathroom.

She didn't know what was going on with Jesse—why, after campaigning relentlessly for her to marry him, he'd been keeping her at arm's length since she'd agreed to do so. Maybe it was another one of those traditions—abstaining from lovemaking until the night of the wedding. Again the horse-and-barn-door analogy came to mind, but she could pretend to be understanding. Because tonight, finally, was their wedding night.

She unzipped her dress the rest of the way and slid it down her body, then hung it on a hook on the back of the door. The snug bodice had eliminated the need for a bra, so she was left in only a pair of lacy bikini panties and thigh-high stockings. She debated for a minute and then removed them, too, before reaching into the bag for the peignoir set her cousin had bought for her.

The sleeveless gown had a soft, stretch lace bodice that dipped low between her breasts, and an empire waist from which fell a long flowing skirt of semi-sheer chiffon. It was feminine and romantic and sexy, and Maggie loved the feel of the soft fabric against her skin. The long-sleeved chiffon wrap had wide lace cuffs and delicate pearl buttons with satin loop closures at the bodice. She slipped her arms into the sleeves but decided to leave the wrap unfastened, then eyed herself critically in the mirror.

Would he see the truth of her feelings for him when he looked at her? Did it matter if he did? She knew he didn't feel the same way, but she couldn't help hoping that maybe, someday, he would.

She was under no illusions about why he wanted to marry her: *it's about giving our baby the family he or she deserves.* He wasn't looking for love, and now—thanks to the conversation she'd overhead in the ladies' room—she knew why. It was because Shaclyn had broken his heart so badly even his mother had worried that he'd never get over her.

She pushed the conversation between those unknown women to the back of her mind. Maybe Jesse's former fiancée had come back to Rust Creek Falls hoping to lasso her cowboy once again, but he'd sent her away and married Maggie. Even if he didn't love her, she knew he cared about her and he loved their baby. That was a pretty good starting point, and she wasn't going to let anything or anyone ruin her wedding night.

They'd shared a connection in the bedroom, and she was confident they would reconnect tonight. She craved not just the physical joining but the emotional intimacy they'd shared; she wanted to make love with him, to show him the true depth of her feelings with her lips and her hands and her body. But she would hold on to the words until he was ready not just to hear them but to believe them.

With her heart pounding against her ribs, she opened the door and stepped out of the bathroom.

"Jesse?"

She tapped her knuckles on the partially closed bedroom door. There was no response. She pushed it open and found the room was empty. His tuxedo was draped over the back of the chair in his bedroom, but her husband was nowhere to be found.

She made her way down the stairs, past his dark office, through the quiet kitchen to the empty living room.

"Jesse?" she said again.

It was then that she noticed his boots and coat were missing from the hook by the back door.

He was gone.

Her husband had left her alone on their wedding night.

Or maybe she was being melodramatic. He'd probably expected it would take her longer to get ready for bed, and he'd decided to go out to the barn to check on the horses while he was waiting. Her spirits buoyed by this thought, she went back upstairs. It was then that she noticed a light spilling out of the doorway of one of the spare bedrooms farther down the hall.

She pushed open the door and found her suitcases neatly aligned at the foot of the bed, undeniable evidence that her husband didn't plan on sharing a bed with her tonight—or anytime in the near future.

She felt the sting of tears behind her eyes as hurt and confusion battled inside of her.

Had she been so blinded by her own feelings that she'd misinterpreted what she'd believed was evidence of his desire for her? How were they supposed to make their marriage work if they were sleeping in separate rooms? And why had he insisted on marrying her if he didn't want to be with her?

Of course she didn't have the answers to any of these questions. All she had was an aching emptiness in her heart, and all she could do was slip between the cold sheets of a bed that wouldn't be shared with her husband and cry herself to sleep.

The next morning, Maggie's first as Jesse's wife, she woke up as she'd fallen asleep: alone.

She climbed out of bed and headed for the bathroom. After she'd washed her face and brushed her teeth, she stepped into the hallway. The scent of fresh coffee wafted up the stairs, luring her to the kitchen. Jesse wasn't there, but the empty cereal bowl and mug in the sink confirmed that he was up—and probably already out in the barn. Rumor around town was that Jesse Crawford liked animals more than he liked people, but Maggie hadn't believed it was true. At least not until he'd left her alone on their wedding night.

She opened three different cupboards before she found the mugs. Although she'd severely cut back on her caffeine consumption as soon as she knew she was pregnant, she still needed half a cup of coffee at the start of the day to feel human in the morning.

She looked out the window over the sink, slowly sipping her coffee and wondering if she might catch a glimpse of her husband. She didn't see him, but she heard the back door open and then close, indicating that he'd returned to the house.

As his footsteps came toward the kitchen, her heart started to pound a little bit faster. But she kept her eyes focused on the window, not wanting to appear overly eager to see him.

"Good mor—" The greeting halted as abruptly as the footsteps.

Her curiosity piqued, Maggie slowly turned to face him, and caught his gaze—hungry and heated—skimming over her.

"What—" He swallowed. "What are you wearing?"

She'd forgotten about the ensemble she'd donned in anticipation of her husband taking it off for her on their wedding night. Had she been thinking about anything but how much she wanted her daily half cup of coffee, she might have covered up. But the blatant masculine appreciation in his eyes warmed every inch of her—from the top of her head to the bare toes on the ceramic tile floor—and made her glad that she hadn't.

"It's called a peignoir set," she told him. "Lissa bought it for me."

He continued to stare at her, as if he couldn't tear his eyes away, but when he spoke, his tone was gruff. "Your cousin should know by now that the winter nights are cold in this part of the country. You'd be better off with something a little less see-through and a little more flannel."

Flannel—as if separate bedrooms wasn't a big enough hint that he didn't want her.

Except that he hadn't looked at her as if he didn't want her. Even now, even though he was staying on the far side of the kitchen, there was something in his gaze—and it wasn't disinterest.

But she only nodded in answer to his statement. "I guess I'm going to have to do some shopping."

He moved to the fridge and yanked on the door handle. "I can't ignore my responsibilities to take you around the shops today."

She blinked, sincerely baffled by his response. "I didn't ask you to take me anywhere."

He dropped a package of bacon on the counter. "No," he finally acknowledged. "I guess you didn't."

That did it. Maggie put her mug on the counter with a thud. "What's going on, Jesse?"

"What do you mean?" He set a frying pan on the stove, turned on the flame beneath it.

"We've barely been married—" she glanced at the clock "—fifteen hours, and you're acting like you're sorry you ever proposed."

"I'm not," he said quickly. "You know this is what I wanted."

"I *thought* it was what you wanted," she acknowledged. "But clearly I'm having trouble reading your signals, because when you asked me to marry you, I didn't think you intended for us to sleep in separate bedrooms."

He opened the bacon, peeled off several strips and placed them in the pan. "When you accepted my proposal, you didn't say you wanted to share a bed," he countered.

"I'm carrying your baby," she reminded him. "And there was nothing immaculate about the conception."

"We've done some things out of order in our relationship," he said, keeping his gaze focused on his task as he moved the slices of bacon around with a fork. "I just thought we should take some time now to get to know one another."

She tried to think about what he was saying objectively. The words sounded reasonable—considerate, even. But she couldn't help but wonder when exactly he'd decided they should take this time: Before or after he'd seen Shaelyn?

Maybe seeing the woman he'd once loved had made him realize he'd made a mistake in proposing to Maggie. But if that was true—why hadn't he called off the wedding?

"If it's so important to you that we take time to get to know one another, why didn't you want to take that time *before* we got married?"

He shrugged. "I wanted to make sure our baby would be born to parents who were legally married."

She nodded. From the moment he'd learned that she was pregnant, he'd been clear that the baby was his primary concern. Maybe his only concern.

What I want—what you want—isn't as important as what our baby needs.

She'd accepted his proposal because she'd been certain that there was more between them than their baby. She'd believed that their relationship was founded on mutual attraction and growing affection.

Now she knew the truth. Jesse didn't want her—he only wanted their baby.

If her silence wasn't evidence enough that he'd said something wrong, the white-knuckle grip in which Maggie held her cup further substantiated the fact.

He'd never been good with words—or relationships, but he'd never had so much at stake before. He decided a shift in topic toward something less personal was warranted.

"Did you have breakfast?" he asked.

She shook her head. "No. I'm not hungry."

"You have to eat," he admonished. "Skipping meals isn't good for the baby."

Apparently he'd said the wrong thing again, because when he glanced up, he saw that her eyes shone with telltale moisture.

Damn. His brain scrambled for something, *anything,* to divert the ensuing flood of tears and recriminations, but he came up empty.

To his surprise—and relief—Maggie lifted her chin. "You're right." She took a banana from the bowl of fruit on the counter. "I'm going to check my email."

And then she was gone, and he didn't know whether he was relieved or disappointed.

The only thing that was certain was that he'd lost his mind—most likely sometime between the minister proclaiming he and Maggie to be husband and wife and his return to the house to make breakfast this morning. It was the only possible reason that might explain why he'd suggested his wife should sleep in something less see-through and more flannel.

Not that what she'd been wearing was exactly seethrough, but the morning light coming through the window had backlit her so that her silhouette was clearly visible. And those delicious curves had tempted him to touch, to trace her feminine contours and revel in the satiny softness of her skin. He'd had to curl his fingers into his palms to prevent himself from reaching out for her. And then she'd turned to face him, and the outline of her peaked nipples pressed against the gauzy fabric had actually made his mouth water.

The first time he saw her, he wanted her. In the five months that had passed since their initial meeting, he hadn't stopped wanting her. And being with Maggie had escalated rather than satiated his desire.

She was right—he hadn't planned on separate bedrooms when he'd asked her to marry him. He couldn't think of anything he wanted as much as he wanted Maggie in his bed again—just imagining her naked body wrapped around his was enough to make him ache. He'd been eager for their wedding day to conclude so that their wedding night could begin. And then he'd been cornered by her brother at the reception.

His conversation with Shane Roarke had made him realize that he'd pushed Maggie into this marriage because it was what *he* wanted. He hadn't asked what she wanted. In fact, he'd ignored her efforts to tell him.

On more than a few occasions, he'd been accused of being stubborn and single-minded, because he rarely gave up until he got what he wanted. And usually the end justified the means—except that, in this situation, he wasn't entirely sure what "end" he wanted. Why had he insisted on this marriage? To ensure he would have a place in his child's life? Or to hold on to Maggie?

Because he didn't know the answers to those questions, and because he wasn't comfortable acknowledging the possibility that he might have pushed her into a marriage she wasn't ready for, he'd forced himself to take a step back.

The fact that she'd slept in that—what had she called it?—peignoir set, suggested that she hadn't planned on sleeping alone.

But the weight of her brother's words continued to echo in the back of his mind.

He'd never even taken Maggie out on a date. They'd gone from introductions to intercourse in a matter of hours. They'd both been on the same page, had both wanted the same thing, but their compatibility in the bedroom aside, what did he really know about her?

After she'd gone back to LA, they'd had several long

telephone conversations, they'd exchanged emails, they'd planned to get together again. But it hadn't happened.

Weeks and then months had passed, and he'd been certain their relationship was over. If what they'd shared could even be categorized as a relationship. After a few more weeks, he'd even managed to convince himself that he didn't care. Yeah, and that conviction had lasted right up until he'd looked up and saw her standing outside the paddock where he was working with Rocky.

He'd been genuinely happy to see her—and mad at himself for being so happy. She'd unceremoniously dumped him, and then reappeared out of nowhere, and his heart had practically leaped out of his chest.

Now, only two weeks later, they were married.

He didn't doubt that they'd done the right thing for their child. Whether it was right for him and Maggie remained to be seen.

Chapter Eleven

Over the next few days, Maggie and Jesse started to become accustomed to living together—albeit as roommates rather than husband and wife. They shared conversation and ate their meals together, but it was all superficial.

They talked mostly about the weather, which Jesse described as alternately chilly/nippy/frosty/blustery or simply cold, and which Maggie interpreted as unbelievably mind-numbingly and bone-chillingly frigid, and the local news: old Mr. Effingham slipped outside of the post office and broke his hip; six-foot-five-inch local basketball star Wendell Holmes was caught with his girlfriend in a compromising position in the backseat of a Chevy Spark at the high school; three ranch hands spent a night in lockup after the most recent brawl at the Ace in the Hole; and Tom Riddell's yellow lab had given birth to a litter of puppies that confirmed the doggy daddy was Liza Weichelt's German shepherd, despite her repeated assertions that Rex never showed any interest in Taffy. The discussion of which might have been more interesting if Maggie knew any of the people involved.

Maggie did most of the cooking, because she enjoyed it, and Jesse did the cleanup. And as they went about their respective duties, he didn't touch her—either by accident or design. It was as if every movement he made was deliberately intended to ensure there was no contact between them. If she asked him to pass the salt, he put the shaker in front of her plate rather than in her hand. If she needed help reaching something on the top shelf of the pantry, he'd wait until she moved aside rather than reach over her.

On Wednesday morning, just four days after her wedding, Maggie was scheduled to start working for Ben Dalton. She woke up early—both nervous and excited about her first day.

Although she'd learned a lot in her tenure with Alliston & Blake, she'd also had almost limitless resources at her disposal. At Ben's office, there weren't a dozen other junior associates to ask for help, there was no senior associate assigned to review her work. There was only Ben, his secretary, Jessica Evanson, and his paralegal, Mallory Franklin. Which meant that if she didn't know how to do something, she would have to ask her boss.

She hoped she didn't have to ask her boss, because she really wanted to make a good impression.

She knew that the people of Rust Creek Falls were reserving judgment—that they were wary of outsiders and didn't trust her not to run out on Jesse the way his former fiancée had done. Only time would convince them of that. She was more concerned with proving that she was smart and capable and independent of the man she'd married.

Ben had confided that he was usually in the office before eight-thirty, but he told her that she could start at nine. Since she was accustomed to early hours and Jesse was up as well, she decided she might as well head into town. She pulled into the small parking lot beside the building at eight-twenty-two and found Ben's Suburban was already there.

She picked up her briefcase and drew in a deep breath, trying to calm the butterflies that were swooping around in her tummy. Apparently it was early for most of the townsfolk, as the streets were quiet. Quite a different scenario from the nearby ranches, where the men would have been up at the crack of dawn, feeding stock and mucking out stalls and whatever else ranch hands did at the start of the day.

Jesse always began his morning at The Shooting Star. After he'd taken care of the animals there, he'd drive over to Traub Stables, where he'd put in several hours training other people's horses. She didn't know what exactly it was that he did, but she knew that when people spoke his name, they did so with respect. Aside from the fact that he had an undeniable gift when it came to animals, he was also universally regarded as a good man.

Maggie didn't disagree, but she would add *enigmatic*, *confusing* and *frustrating* to his list of attributes. And apparently, since their marriage, *celibate*—which contributed in no small part to the *frustrating*.

As she made her way around the building, she was startled to find Homer Gilmore sitting on the bottom step that led to the front door of the law office. She'd seen him around town before, but she didn't know much about him. She didn't put much stock in gossip or rumor, although the consensus was that he was a crazy old coot. She thought *lost* was a more apt description, as if he wasn't quite sure where he was or how he got there, but he seemed harmless. Certainly she'd never had reason to fear him, so she greeted him pleasantly now.

"Good morning, Mr. Gilmore."

He scrambled up from the step and moved out of her way. "The past is the present."

She wasn't sure if the mumbled words were intended as some kind of cryptic response to her greeting or if he was talking to himself.

"It's a little chilly this morning," she said, making her

way up the steps. Actually, it was more than chilly by LA standards, but she knew that saying so would only highlight her status as an outsider.

"The past is the present."

"O-kay."

"The past is the present." He muttered the same statement again, so quickly now the words almost ran together.

"Well," she kept her tone cheerful, "I should get in to work."

"Thepastisthepresent."

She opened the door and stepped into the outer office, concerned that the rumors about his sanity might be true.

Maggie spent the first hour and a half in her new office reviewing the client files her boss had put on her desk for later discussion. Jessica arrived just before nine and settled at her desk; Mallory came in a few minutes later, after she'd taken her niece Lily to school.

Everyone seemed to have their own routines and enough work to keep occupied—except for Maggie.

Just before ten o'clock, Ben Dalton knocked on her open door. "I've got a settlement conference in Kalispell," he said. "If you want to come with me, I can introduce you to the court staff and some of the local Bar members."

"I'd like that," she agreed readily.

On the way, he gave her some background information about the issues to be discussed, his client—an employer trying to negotiate an agreement with a former employee—the opposing counsel and the judge who was scheduled to preside over the conference.

Afterward, they went for lunch and while they were waiting for their food to be delivered, they discussed the files Ben had asked her to review. One was an application for a variation of a custody agreement, another was a landlord-tenant dispute and the third was a breach of contract case. Maggie had not just familiarized herself with the details of the cases but made notes of relevant statutes and precedents for each.

Ben seemed pleased with her initiative and insights, and confided that he'd been thinking about expanding his practice for a few years. Hiring Mallory Franklin as a paralegal had been the first step, and because she now did a lot of the paperwork that he used to do, he was able to keep more regular hours than he had in years. He hadn't given up on his plan to bring in a second lawyer, but there hadn't been any qualified candidates in Rust Creek Falls—until Maggie.

"With your background and experience, we can expand the services offered to our clients," he told her.

"I'm looking forward to being able to help," she said.

Ben nodded. "And maybe we can even work out some kind of partnership agreement after you pass the Montana Bar, so that you can work with me instead of for me."

Maggie stared across the table at him, too stunned to reply.

"What do you think—should it be Dalton & Roarke or Dalton & Crawford?"

She hadn't thought about whether she would take Jesse's name professionally. As for a partnership, she hadn't thought about that at all.

"Or maybe that's more responsibility than you're looking for?" he asked, when she didn't respond.

"No," she said quickly. "That's *exactly* the kind of responsibility I'm looking for.

"I guess I'm just…surprised," she admitted. "I worked more than sixty hours a week for years at Alliston & Blake before there was any mention of a promotion, and I haven't even worked here for six hours and you're offering me the possibility of a partnership."

"You think a small-town Montana lawyer doesn't have sense to know what he's doing?"

"On the contrary, I think you're a lot smarter than any of my bosses in Los Angeles."

He chuckled. "And I like to think you'd be right. I did my research," he assured her. "Beyond the work experience that was outlined on your résumé, I know that you graduated in the top five percent of your class from Stanford Law and passed the California Bar on your first try. In addition to the sixty-plus hours a week that you worked at your firm, you somehow found time to be an active member of the Women Lawyer's Association of Los Angeles and volunteer at a local women's shelter."

"That's pretty thorough research," she noted.

"I assure you, Maggie, I didn't hire you on a whim because your husband works for my son-in-law or because your cousin is married to the sheriff. I hired you because I want to expand the range of legal services available to the people of Rust Creek Falls and because I want to know this firm will be in capable hands when I decide to retire."

"Then I guess we should talk about the specific areas of expansion," she said, already looking forward to it.

Jesse spent the majority of his time at Traub Stables with the horses, but he always ended his day in front of the computer. He made detailed notes of his interactions with every animal and meticulously documented those notes in individual folders on Sutter's computer so they could be easily referenced by the owner.

He was at the computer on Thursday when Sutter strolled into the office with a baby carrier in hand.

Jesse looked over and couldn't help but smile at the wide-eyed infant.

"Good-looking kid," he said. "Must take after his mama."

Sutter chuckled, unoffended. "That he does. But his mama had a meeting at the school today, so the men are hanging out together."

"Drinking beer and smoking cigars?"

"Maybe in a few more years."

"Good call," Jesse told him.

"I hear you're going to have a baby of your own in a few months."

"News travels," he said, not at all surprised by the fact.

"Are you excited or terrified?"

"Both," Jesse admitted.

"I was, too," Sutter said. "Truthfully, I still am. But I wouldn't give him back for anything in the world."

As he spoke, he set the baby carrier on the desk to pull his cell phone out of his pocket and glance at the display.

"Brooks is here," Sutter said, naming the local vet. "Do you mind if I leave Carter with you while I go talk to him?"

"No problem," Jesse assured him.

"I won't be more than ten minutes," his boss promised.

It was the longest ten minutes of his life.

While Carter had seemed perfectly happy to gurgle and coo while his daddy was in his line of sight, as soon as Sutter walked out of the room, the baby began to squirm and fuss. Jesse tried rocking the carrier, to no avail. The fussing escalated to crying. He unbuckled the straps and lifted Carter out.

The little guy looked at him, his big blue eyes filled with tears, his lower lip trembling.

"Daddy's going to be right back," Jesse promised.

Carter drew in a long, shuddery breath, as if considering whether or not to believe him. But when "right back" was not immediate, the crying started anew.

Jesse tucked him close to his body, the baby squirmed; he cradled him in the crook of his arm—a favorite position of his niece Noelle's when she was younger—the wails grew louder; he propped him up on his shoulder and patted his back. The baby let out a belch surprisingly disproportionate to his size—and the crying began to quiet and, finally, stopped.

"That feels better now, doesn't it, buddy?"

Of course, the baby didn't respond. He let out a long, shuddery sigh, rubbed his cheek against Jesse's shoulder, and his eyes drifted shut.

Jesse couldn't help but smile.

His sister's little girl was the epitome of sugar and spice. She was soft and feminine and heartbreakingly beautiful. Sutter's son, although only four months old, was already snakes and snails. He was solid and sturdy and 100 percent boy.

Jesse hadn't given much thought to the gender of his own baby. When he'd learned that Maggie was pregnant, his primary concern had been marrying her to ensure his place in their baby's life. Now, however—

That thought was severed by the sudden realization that the back of his shirt was wet.

Carter hadn't just released an air bubble—he'd spewed the contents of his stomach all over Jesse.

"Why is there a sticky note on the fridge that says 'burp cloths'?" Maggie asked when Jesse came in for dinner later that night.

"I thought we should start making a list of things we'll need to get before the baby comes," he said.

She eyed him skeptically. "And the first thing that came

to mind wasn't a car seat or crib or even diapers—it was
burp cloths?"

"I spent some time with Sutter and Paige's little guy
today."

"His proud grandpa has shown me about a hundred
pictures," she said.

"He puked all down my back."

She laughed. Then pressed a hand to her lips in a belated
attempt to hide the fact that she was laughing.

His gaze narrowed.

"I'm sorry," she apologized, not sounding sorry at all.
"I'm sure it was disgusting."

"I know that babies puke and poop and cry," he acknowledged. "But it's one thing to read about it in a book
and another to experience firsthand."

"Noelle never puked on you?"

He shook his head. "She's spit up a little, but nothing
more than that."

Maggie put a plate of chicken parm on the table in
front of him.

"How was your day?" he asked her.

"Well, I didn't have to deal with any puking babies."
She sat down across from him with her own plate. "In fact,
I didn't have to do much of anything.

"Ben took me to Kalispell for an arbitration today.
We chatted on the drive, lingered over coffee when we
got there, he presented his case to the arbitrator, then we
had lunch and returned to Rust Creek Falls around three
o'clock, at which point he decided we'd done enough for
the day."

"Most people would be happy to finish their day at three
o'clock," he pointed out to her.

"I know. I just felt kind of…useless," she admitted. "Ben

promised he'd make me earn my salary, but I'm not sure that will happen until I pass the Bar."

"Maybe you need to remind yourself that you're not in LA anymore and relax a little bit," he suggested.

"That's what Ben said," she admitted.

"Imagine… I gave the same advice as an attorney without charging two hundred dollars an hour for it."

"Which is less than half the rate of most lawyers in California. Of course, the cost of office space is a lot higher there, too."

"Do you miss it?"

She shook her head. "Having time on my hands is a new experience but I think, once I get used to it, I'll enjoy the slower pace and lessened pressure. And I really like Ben and Mallory and Jessica—I'm not sure I could say that about any of the people I worked with at Alliston & Blake. I'm sure they were all great people, but I was so busy focusing on my clients and cases that I never really got to know any of them very well."

"I didn't have the chance to get to know your boss very well, but I'm sure I didn't like him," Jesse told her.

"Brian was always fond of saying he was in the business of business, not making friends."

"That's probably one of the reasons I prefer to work with animals than people." He pushed away from the table and carried his empty plate to the sink.

She appreciated that Jesse always insisted on doing the dishes if she did the cooking, but she wished he didn't shoo her out of the kitchen so that he could do the cleaning up. She just wanted to be with him, to do the things that most married couples did together. And since—for reasons she still didn't understand—that didn't include sex at the present, she was so pathetically eager to spend time with him she would settle for sharing chores.

She began to clear away the rest of the table. When she picked up a towel to dry the dishes he'd already washed, Jesse said, "I'll do that."

But this time, she didn't let him ban her from the room. "I don't mind," she told him.

Short of wrestling the towel from her, there was nothing he could do, so he shrugged and focused his attention on the washing again. He didn't say anything while he completed the chore, but she didn't mind the silence.

She put the last pot back in the cupboard then turned to hang the towel on the oven handle. She hadn't realized he was right behind her, and when she turned, her breasts brushed against his chest. The shock of the contact might have jolted her backward, except that the counter was at her back and Jesse was at her front, so she had nowhere to go.

She lifted her gaze to his and saw both heat and hunger reflected in his eyes. Her heart pounded harder and faster and her mouth went dry. The atmosphere crackled with heat and tension. She instinctively moistened her lips, and his eyes darkened as they followed the movement of her tongue. His gaze shifted from her mouth to her breasts, zeroing in on nipples that were already peaked, begging for his attention.

Jesse drew in a slow, deep breath. Then he took a deliberate step back, away from her.

"I have to go out…to check on Lancelot."

She swallowed, torn between frustration and disappointment. "Now?"

"Nate asked me to take a look at him—said he was favoring his right foreleg."

She nodded, because she could hardly dispute the importance of checking on an injured animal.

But as she watched him grab his coat and walk out the

back door, she wondered if she'd have to grow a tail and a mane to make him take a look at her.

And so it went for the next several days—except that Maggie banned herself from the kitchen after dinner. She didn't mind playing with fire, but she hated being the only one who felt the burn.

She tried to talk to her cousin, in the hope that Lissa might have some insights into Jesse's behavior. But although Lissa was puzzled by the distance he was deliberately keeping from his bride, she had no words of wisdom except to say that no man could resist a woman intent on seduction—especially if that woman was his wife.

The problem was that Maggie didn't know the first thing about seduction. She could count the number of lovers she'd had on one hand, with two fingers left over.

The first had been the editor of the law review. She'd fallen in love with his mind and decided that she liked the rest of him well enough to take their relationship to the next level. But the actual event, when it finally happened, was less than spectacular. Still, they'd stayed together for another four months before the relationship eventually fizzled away.

The second had been a former client at Alliston & Blake. She'd never actually worked with him, but she'd been in the elevator when he'd left a meeting with David Connors, one of the senior IP attorneys. He'd asked her to have dinner with him; she'd declined, telling him that it was against company policy for attorneys to fraternize with clients. He'd responded by calling David Connors on his cell phone, right then and there, and firing him. They'd dated for almost a year, and while the physical aspect of their relationship had been pleasant enough, he hadn't exactly rocked her world.

No one had—until Jesse.

She didn't know if the sex had been so great because she felt a deep, emotional connection that she'd never experienced with anyone else, or if she felt a deep, emotional connection to him because the sex had been so great.

Or maybe it hadn't been as great as she remembered... Or maybe it had been great for her but not for him... Or maybe she should stop driving herself crazy speculating about things and figure out what was keeping her husband so busy he was out of the house more than in it.

Because it seemed that every night he had one excuse or another to escape from the house right after dinner. If she'd still been working at Alliston & Blake, she wouldn't have minded being married to a man who was absent for frequent and extended periods—she probably wouldn't even have noticed.

A glance at her watch revealed that it was just past eight o'clock. Jesse's truck was parked out front, so she knew that he hadn't gone far.

She put on her boots and bundled into her coat, wrapping her scarf around her throat, tugging a hat onto her head and slipping thick mittens over her hands. She didn't know if she'd ever get used to Montana temperatures, but she was learning to cope with them.

It helped if she didn't check the daily forecast for LA, as she'd done that morning, only to discover that it was sixty-four degrees in SoCal—forty degrees warmer than in Rust Creek Falls. No wonder she hadn't owned a winter coat until she'd gone shopping in Kalispell with Lissa before the wedding. Unlike the peignoir set her cousin had purchased for her, she actually used the coat.

Her breath puffed out in little clouds, and the snow crunched under her feet as she made her way toward the stables. It wasn't a long trek from the house, but her cheeks and nose were numb by the time she reached the door. The light inside gave her hope that she would find her husband there.

The scent of hay and horses no longer filled her with panic. Instead, it reminded her of Jesse's kiss—the comfort of his arms around her, the warmth of his mouth against hers—and renewed her determination to track down her errant husband.

Honey poked her head over the gate when Maggie ventured near. She was tempted to go closer, to rub the animal's long nose the way Jesse had taught her, but she wasn't nearly as brave without him beside her. She just kept walking, toward what he'd explained was the birthing stall at the back of the barn and from which the light emanated.

She didn't know what she expected to find him doing—but whatever possibilities had crossed her mind, finding him rubbing sandpaper over a carved piece of wood was not one of them.

She didn't know if she made some kind of sound or if he sensed her standing in the open doorway, but his movements suddenly stilled and he looked up at her.

She stepped into the stall, her curious gaze taking in the assortment of pieces spread out over a large worktable—along with the plans for a baby's cradle.

"Oh." Her heart, already his, went splat at his feet. "Is this why you didn't put *crib* on one of your sticky notes?"

He smiled. "We'll need one eventually, but I wanted to do this."

"I thought horses were your thing."

"They are—but sometimes I like to putter."

She looked at the pieces of wood, meticulously carved and sanded. "You're a very talented putterer."

"Is that even a word?"

"I don't think so," she admitted, running her hand over

what she guessed—based on the picture—was the top of a side rail. But referring to him as a putterer was safer than saying that he was good with his hands. Because he undoubtedly was, but that kind of comment would bring to mind all kinds of things that he could do with his hands, things he had done with his hands, things she wished he would do with his hands again. Pushing those tantalizingly torturous thoughts aside, she asked, "Where did you learn to do this?"

"My grandfather was a carpenter as well as a rancher. He taught me a lot of tricks to working with wood."

"The one who made Noelle's blocks?" she guessed.

He nodded.

"Did he make the blanket chest at the foot of my bed?"

"No. I made that."

She'd thought it was a family heirloom, and knew that someday it would be. Just as this cradle would be enjoyed by their child, and maybe, eventually, their child's child.

"There's something else on your mind," he guessed. "You didn't come out here to talk about puttering."

She managed a smile. "No, because I didn't know about the puttering until I got out here."

"Something you want to talk about?"

"I'm not sure," she admitted.

He picked up a soft cloth and began to wipe down the sanded pieces in preparation for staining. "When you decide, you can let me know."

It would be easier, she decided, to ask the question when he wasn't looking at her. When he couldn't see the doubts and insecurities she feared might be reflected in her eyes.

So with his attention focused on his task, she blurted out, "Why didn't you tell me your ex-fiancée was in town?"

Chapter Twelve

Jesse looked up, sincerely startled by the question. "I didn't know that she was."

"I don't mean today," Maggie amended. "I meant the day we got married."

"Oh."

"Why didn't you tell me?" she asked again.

"Because I didn't think it was important."

"The woman you were once planning to marry shows up in town on the day of our wedding and you don't think it's important?"

He sighed. "I don't know how much you know about that engagement—"

"As much as you've told me, which is nothing."

"Because there isn't much to tell. We were engaged for a few weeks—not even long enough to plan a wedding."

"That's longer than we were engaged," she pointed out.

"What do you want me to say, Maggie?"

"I don't know," she admitted. "But I guess I've been wondering... Are you still in love with her?"

"No." His response was immediate and unequivocal.

She didn't look convinced.

"The truth is, I hadn't seen her in almost seven years," he told her. "And I never knew if seeing her again might stir up any old feelings. But it didn't. Any feelings I once had for her are long gone."

"Well, I guess that's good," she said. "Considering that you're now married to me."

"And I'm happy to be married to you."

She opened her mouth, then closed it again without saying a word.

"If there's something you want to say, just say it," Jesse suggested. "I'm not a mind reader."

"One of the first things a lawyer learns is to never ask a question that she doesn't already know the answer to."

"Was it a legal question you were wondering about?"

"No," she admitted. "But in this situation, I think the same rule applies."

He decided to ask a question of his own. "How did you find out about Shaelyn's visit?"

"I overheard some women talking about it at our reception."

"Why didn't you ask me about it then?"

"Because I was hoping you would tell me about it," she admitted.

"I didn't tell you because I forgot about her the minute she walked out the door."

She had no reason not to believe what he was telling her, but his casual dismissal of his former fiancée made her wonder if, during the four months that he and Maggie had been apart, he'd forgotten about her just as easily.

If she hadn't been pregnant, she might not have seen him again. She wouldn't have had any reason to seek him out, and he hadn't shown any inclination to track her down. They were only together now because of their baby—and while she was exactly where she wanted to be, she wasn't convinced the same was true for Jesse.

"I'm sorry I interrupted your work," she said.

"I didn't mind the interruption," he told her. "But you kind of ruined the surprise."

"I'll be surprised when it's all put together," she promised him, heading toward the door.

"Maggie—"

She paused with her fingers wrapped around the handle and turned back.

"I don't want to be with anyone but you," he told her.

She managed a smile. "Same goes."

As she headed back to the house, she told herself that she should be satisfied. He wanted to be with her, and that should be enough.

But it wasn't—she wanted him to love her as much as she loved him.

At Alliston & Blake, there was an office manager in charge of ensuring supplies were documented and maintained. At Ben's office, Jessica usually went into Kalispell once a month to replenish supplies as required. If anything was needed in the interim, it could usually be obtained from the General Store.

Which was why Maggie was at Crawford's to pick up a package of printer paper on Friday afternoon. Natalie directed her to the stationery section at the back of the store, where she found Nina pacing with Noelle in her arms.

"Someone doesn't look too happy today," she said, noting the runny nose and teary eyes of the little girl in her mother's arms.

"That's why my sister's working the register and I'm hiding out back here," Nina admitted.

"Is she sick?" Maggie asked.

"Teething," her sister-in-law clarified. "She's been teething for six months—but every new tooth seems to make her grumpier than the previous one."

Maggie stroked the back of a finger over the child's red cheek. Noelle looked at her and let out a shuddery sigh.

"I was just about to take her upstairs to see if she'll nap," Nina said. "Do you have time for a cup of tea?"

Maggie glanced at her watch, although, aside from printing the memorandum she'd drafted and which didn't need to be submitted until Monday, she had absolutely nothing pressing at the office. "I do if you do," she told her sister-in-law.

Nina led the way through the store to the staircase behind women's sleepwear.

"I lived up here before I moved in with Dallas. Because I manage the store, it was convenient. I decided to keep the apartment, at least for now, so that Noelle can be close by when I'm working. It makes it easy for me to slip away to nurse her—or take a nap with her."

"You're nursing even while she's teething?"

"For now," Nina agreed. "We've been supplementing with formula for a few months, because it gives me a little more freedom, but they say that breast milk is best for the first year, so even when I'm not nursing, I'm pumping."

The door opened into a big living room that was separated from the kitchen and dining area by an island counter. It was bright and spacious but as warm and inviting as the woman who had decorated it.

"This is nice," Maggie said sincerely.

"I like it," Nina said. "It was where I originally planned on living with Noelle—until I fell in love with Dallas. Now he's going to add on to his house—our house—so that we'll have a master suite on the main level and then the current master bedroom can be divided into two rooms and each of the kids will have their own."

"Are you planning to add to your family?" Maggie asked.

"I think four is a good number." Nina passed the baby to her sister-in-law so that she could make tea. "But I have to admit, I've been thinking that it would be nice to have a baby with Dallas."

"What does he say about that?"

"It took some getting used to for him with Noelle. Robbie is seven now, so dealing with midnight feedings and dirty diapers was a big adjustment for him, so I haven't even mentioned the idea yet. I was thinking I'd give him a little more time before I bring up the subject—and to make sure it isn't just a whim on my part."

Watching Nina's ease with and obvious love for her baby, Maggie didn't think it was a whim. Jesse's sister was clearly one of those women who was meant to be a mother, and she knew that her husband was lucky to have found a woman who loved the children from his first marriage as much as she loved her own.

"Speaking of homes," Nina said. "Did you know that Jesse built his? Well, not by himself," she clarified. "My dad and my brothers helped."

"He didn't tell me." But the information reminded her that she'd wondered about something else. "How long has he lived there?"

"Four years, I think." And then, demonstrating a startling insight into her sister-in-law's mind, she said, "It was definitely post-Shaelyn."

Maggie nodded, grateful for the information. "Did he design it, too?"

"Inside and out," Nina confirmed.

"He's got a good eye—and great hands."

"Please," Nina said. "There are some details a sister doesn't need to know."

Maggie felt as if her cheeks were as red as Noelle's. "I meant that he's good with tools."

Her sister-in-law raised a brow.

She blew out a breath. "I saw the cradle he's making for the baby."

"He's making a cradle?" Nina's eyes misted. "That's so sweet—and so Jesse."

"Is it?"

"He's over the moon about this baby."

Maggie looked down at the little girl now sleeping in her arms. "I'm pretty excited, too. I can't wait to hold my own baby just like this."

"He—or she—will be here before you know it, and then what you'll want more than anything in the world is a few hours of uninterrupted sleep."

"I'm sure that's true," Maggie agreed. "But I still can't wait. Of course, I'm as terrified as I am excited, but since there's no turning back now, I'm trying to focus on the positive."

Nina was silent for a minute, seemingly content to just watch Maggie cuddle with Noelle. But when she spoke again, the sincere concern in her tone even more than the question warned Maggie that the other woman suspected all was not wedded bliss for her brother and sister-in-law.

"Is everything okay?" she asked gently.

Maggie managed a smile, in an effort to convince Nina as well as herself. "Everything's great."

"The day that you and Jesse got married, you were absolutely glowing," Nina said. "You're not glowing anymore."

Since Maggie couldn't dispute that, she said nothing.

"Are you unhappy here?" her sister-in-law prompted.

"No. I'm really coming to love Rust Creek Falls."

"Are you missing your family?"

"Sure," she admitted. "But I'm building a new family here, with Jesse." When Nina's only response was patient silence, Maggie sighed. "I guess I just hoped that we'd have more time together. He's so busy, between his work at Traub Stables and chores at The Shooting Star, that I hardly ever see him."

Nina's brow furrowed. "I would expect a new husband to make more time for his bride."

"You know why we got married," Maggie reminded her.

"I know why you got married as quickly as you did," her sister-in-law allowed. "I also know that Jesse started to fall for you the first time he saw you—long before there was a baby in the picture."

Maggie was surprised by the statement. What Nina apparently "knew" was news to her.

Yes, Jesse had been attracted to her from the start—which was why there was a baby on the way—but she didn't know if she'd go so far as to say that he'd fallen for her. Even if she'd fallen head over heels for him a long time ago.

"Did he tell you about Shaelyn?" Nina asked.

"Only that he was engaged to her, briefly."

"That's true, but not even close to being the whole truth." She picked up her tea, sipped. "It's not really my place to tell you the story—or at least what I know of it—but I think you should know the basics, so that you won't lose all patience with my idiot brother."

"I'm not sure how to respond to that," Maggie admitted, making Nina laugh.

"You don't have to—as much as I love him, I'm not blind to his faults."

She sipped her tea again while she considered what—or maybe how much—to say. Maggie set aside her own cup, unable to drink her tea while her stomach was twisting itself into knots.

"He loved her," Nina finally said, and with those words, the knots tightened painfully. "In that innocent first love kind of way. You have to understand what it was like for

Jesse growing up in our family. He's always been the quiet one, the more introspective one. And he's sensitive, which is probably why he's so good with animals, and why he doesn't like to play with anyone's emotions.

"All of the local girls chased after Nate and Justin and Brad. Jesse was every bit as good-looking, smart and charming, but he was overlooked because he let himself be.

"When he went away to college, he was no longer competing with our brothers for attention, and the girls started to notice him for who he was. Shaelyn set her sights on him from day one. He didn't have a lot of experience deciphering subtle signals, but there was nothing subtle about Shaelyn."

"You didn't like her," Maggie realized.

"I wanted to—for Jesse's sake. But Shaelyn didn't have many redeeming qualities, aside from the fact that she loved my brother."

"And he loved her."

"He was infatuated," Nina allowed. "I'm not sure it was anything more than that, although he certainly thought it wàs, at least at the time.

"And his experience with Shaelyn did make him wary. So I'm going to ask you to try to be patient with him. To give him the time he needs to accept how he feels about you."

"What if you're wrong about his feelings?"

"I'm not," her sister-in-law promised.

Maggie wished she could be half as certain, but her conversation with Nina had at least given her hope.

Jesse's excited anticipation about the impending birth of his child was tempered by his fear that the baby's mother would wake up one day and realize she hated life in Rust Creek Falls. Because if that happened and Maggie decided to go back to Los Angeles, he'd lose everything that mattered most to him.

It was this fear that kept him from admitting—to her and himself—the true depth of his feelings. It was easy to keep busy around the ranch: mending broken fences, mucking out stalls and working with the horses. But that hadn't taken up all of his time, so he'd decided to build a cradle. It was something he wanted to do, and it gave him an excuse to stay out in the barn, away from Maggie. Because he couldn't be around Maggie without wanting Maggie, and giving in to that want would inevitably tangle up his heart, and he wasn't ready to go down that road again.

Except that he was almost finished the cradle, and he didn't know what project to tackle next. Maybe he would see if he could find a good plan for a crib.

He was assembling the stand when Honey nickered a happy greeting. Curious, he left the worktable and rounded the corner to discover Nina rubbing an affectionate hand down the horse's muzzle.

"What brings you out here?" he asked his sister.

"Maybe I just wanted to see my big brother."

"More likely you want something from your big brother," he guessed. "Like a babysitter?"

She smiled, unoffended by the assumption. "I really just wanted to see how you were doing—how you're settling into married life."

"Fine."

She lifted her brows in response to his single-word answer. "I don't know if I can express how incredibly reassured I am."

"I don't know why you'd need reassurance," he said. "But I'm glad I could help."

"Maggie told me you were making a cradle for the baby."

"When did you see Maggie?"

"She came to the store yesterday?"

"Yesterday?" he echoed incredulously. "And you waited a whole twenty-four hours to track me down to no doubt tell me that my marriage is doomed?"

"I don't think your marriage is doomed," she denied. "Although it's interesting that you would project that forecast onto me."

"I'm not projecting anything."

"Can I see the cradle?"

Happy to turn her attention to something other than his marriage, he led her to the workbench.

"Oh," she said, when he removed the protective cloth he'd draped over it. "Wow. Jesse, this is—" she ran a hand over the smoothly curved footboard "—gorgeous."

"I think it turned out pretty good," he agreed.

"This was obviously a labor of love."

"I wanted the baby to have—"

"This isn't for the baby," she interjected softly. "It's for Maggie."

"I'm pretty sure Maggie won't fit in it."

"You know what I mean," she chided. "This is your way of showing Maggie—because God forbid you should actually use words—how you feel about her."

His only response was to pull the blanket back over the cradle.

Nina sighed. "What are you afraid of?"

"I'm not afraid of anything."

"Good—because she married you, Jesse. She let you put a ring on her finger and she put one on yours and she promised to stay with you 'so long as you both shall live.'"

"Your point?" he prompted.

"You've got to stop waiting for her to leave," she said gently.

He scowled. "I'm not."

"Maybe not consciously, but I know you, and I see the way you look at her—and the way you don't let her see you look at her."

He frowned. "I'm not sure what you just said even makes any sense."

"Okay, I'll put it in simple terms that even you can understand—Maggie isn't Shaelyn. Don't make her pay for what Shaelyn did to you."

"I know she's not Shaelyn."

"Do you?" his sister challenged. "Do you realize that she looks at you as if you're everything she wants and needs? Or do you look at her and think—she's going to hate it here? That after having lived her whole life in Los Angeles, she's never going to adjust to life in Rust Creek Falls?"

"I can't deny that the possibility has crossed my mind, but I'm not waiting for it to happen."

"Here's another question—when you asked her to marry you, did you tell her how you feel about her or did you make it all about the baby?"

"I'm really glad that you're in love and happily married—even if you did choose to marry a Traub—but I don't want or need your marital advice."

She shook her head. "You haven't told her how you feel, have you?"

"Maggie and I both know why we got married."

"I don't think either of you has a clue about the other's reasons."

He scowled at that.

"She's not going to break your heart," Nina told him. "But if you're not careful—or maybe I should say if you don't stop being careful—you might break hers."

"I've got things to do, so if that's all…"

"There is one more thing."

"What is it?" he asked, not bothering to disguise his impatience.

"The holiday pageant at the elementary school is on Monday night. Ryder's part of the stage crew, and Jake and Robbie both have parts. I'd like you and Maggie to come."

"I don't think—"

"Most of Dallas's family has already said that they'll be there," she interjected to cut off what she no doubt knew was going to be a refusal.

He tried again. "I'm not sure a school play is Maggie's kind of thing."

"You might be surprised—by a lot of things."

He scowled. "What's that supposed to mean?"

"It means, ask her," his sister said, heading toward the door. "The show starts at seven."

So Jesse asked her.

When he got back to the house, Maggie was on her computer, looking on Pinterest for decorating ideas for the nursery. Her study manuals for the Bar exam were closed on the table beside her.

"My brain needed a break," she said.

He took a bottle of beer from the fridge, twisted off the cap. "I'm not surprised," he said. "You've been working nonstop since you got here."

"I used to take work home from the office all the time. Now I'm lucky if I have enough work to keep me in the office until five o'clock."

"Are you bored?"

"No, I enjoy what I'm doing. I'm just not accustomed to having so much time on my hands."

He felt another twinge of guilt as he realized it was true. Not only did her job demand fewer hours, but she didn't have the number of friends and acquaintances that she'd had in California. Yes, her cousin, Lissa, was here—but Lissa and Gage were head over heels in love and rarely more than ten feet away from one another.

"Do you have some time Monday night?"

"For what?" she asked, just a little warily.

"There's a Christmas pageant at the elementary school," he explained.

"Actually, it's a holiday pageant."

"Huh?"

"They're billing it as a holiday pageant this year because of the earlier date. There's going to be a short Thanksgiving play, holiday songs performed by the school choir and then the Christmas production."

"How do you know all of this?"

"Ben's daughter Paige teaches at the elementary school. Well, she's not teaching right now because she just had the baby, but she was talking about it when she came into the office last week. The earlier date—apparently a result of Winona Cobbs forecasting some big snowstorm—left the teachers scrambling to get everything ready on time."

He chuckled. "She's forecasting a big snowstorm?"

"You think she's wrong?" she asked hopefully.

"I think winter snowstorms in Montana are inevitable."

She sighed. "Obviously I'm going to need more than one pair of long johns."

She was making a joke—at least, he thought she was joking—but just the mention of her needing more long johns started him thinking about her nonthermal underwear. He'd had the pleasure of undressing her a few times now and he remembered—in scorching detail—that she liked to match her panties and her bras. But even more tempting were the feminine treasures he'd discovered hidden within the delicate scraps of lace.

"About the pageant," he prompted, in a desperate attempt to get his own thoughts back on track. "Do you want to go?"

"Sure," she agreed. "But why do you sound less than enthusiastic?"

"It's not exactly my idea of fun."

"Then why did you ask me to go?"

"Because misery loves company, and Nina guilted me into going."

"How did she do that?"

"She said that all of the Traubs were going to be there."

"So?"

"You know about the rivalry between the Crawfords and the Traubs," he reminded her.

"I thought Nina and Dallas getting married had put an end to all of that."

"Their wedding might have started to bridge the divide," Jesse allowed. "But the tension between the two families is still there, beneath the surface, with this ongoing one-upmanship. If Dallas's family is all going to be there, then Nina's family all needs to be there to show that we're just as supportive as they are."

"Sounds...exhausting," Maggie decided.

"Yeah," he agreed. "And mostly I don't care, but since Nina asked..."

"You feel obligated."

He nodded. "But if you don't want to—"

"I'm not going to be your excuse for begging off," she told him.

"I wasn't going to use you as an excuse, but only because I didn't think of it," he admitted. "I was just going to say that you aren't under the same obligation, so if you don't want to go, you don't have to."

"And give your parents another reason not to like me?" She shook her head. "I don't think so."

He frowned. "My parents don't dislike you."

"They think I trapped you into marrying me."

"No, they don't," he denied, uncomfortable to realize that she believed such a thing, and that he'd done nothing to reassure her. "They do have some concerns about the fact that we got married quickly and don't know each other very well, but they'll come around."

"Before or after our child graduates from college?"

He smiled at her wry tone. "Hopefully before."

"Well, in the meantime, I would like to go to the holiday pageant with you."

"You would?"

"Sure," she agreed. "What time does it start?"

"Seven o'clock. But we should probably be there by six-thirty if we want to get a seat in the auditorium."

"Are you expecting the show to sell out?"

"There's not a lot of entertainment in Rust Creek Falls," he reminded her.

Chapter Thirteen

It hadn't taken Maggie long to realize the trick to tolerating the frigid Montana weather was layers. Lots of layers. So she started with long johns under her dark jeans and a long-sleeved knit top beneath a bulky cable-knit sweater in pale pink. Then she added some dangly earrings, just for fun.

She didn't miss the cocktail parties and dinner meetings that were so much a part of her life in LA, but she did miss dressing up and feeling pretty. In need of a little extra boost, she added mascara to her lashes and a darker than usual shade of gloss to her lips.

Jesse was ready and waiting for her when she came downstairs. He'd showered and changed into a clean pair of jeans with a dark blue V-neck sweater over a lighter blue crewneck T-shirt. He hadn't bothered to shave, and the dark shadow on his cheeks and jaw made him look even more rugged and sexy—and made her heart slam against her ribs.

It was the closest thing they'd ever had to a date. She wondered if he would hold her hand, and chided herself for the flutters of anticipation that danced in her tummy.

She'd had sex with him—more than once even, but not at all since their wedding—and now she was desperate for any sign of interest or affection.

Sometimes when he looked at her, she thought she saw

a flicker of heat, a glimpse of desire, but then he'd look away, leaving her to wonder if she'd only imagined it. She didn't understand why he'd pushed so hard for her to marry him, and then completely withdrawn once his ring was on her finger.

He looked at her, his gaze skimming from the boots on her feet to the top of her head, lingering at certain spots in a way that made her breasts ache and her thighs tingle. But when he spoke, it was only to say, "You're going to want a hat. It's cold outside."

"It's November in Montana—of course it's cold outside," she noted drily. But she found the new pink hat and matching gloves she'd bought on a recent trip into Kalispell and put them on.

"How many hats do you own?"

"Hopefully enough."

"You do know that you can only wear one at a time?" he teased, flicking the pom-pom on top of her head.

"I like to accessorize."

"You look good in pink," he told her.

She was surprised—and pleased—by the compliment.

"And in skirts," he said. "Although I haven't seen you in one since we got married."

"And you probably won't until spring," she warned. "There's no way I'm baring my legs in this weather."

"That's too bad—because yours are spectacular. Especially when you wear those heels that make them look a mile long."

The comment seemed to surprise him as much as it surprised her. But she kept her tone light when she said, "So you're a leg man, are you?"

"I like *your* legs," he admitted, his gaze skimming down her body, then slowly up again. "Actually, I like every part of you."

"Really?"

"You're a beautiful woman, Maggie," he said.

She blew out an unsteady breath. "And you're a confusing man."

He held her gaze for a long minute, as if there was something more he wanted to say. But in the end, he only asked, "Are you ready to go?"

As soon as they got to the doors of the auditorium, Maggie realized that Jesse had not exaggerated the popularity of the event. Although there was still more than half an hour before the pageant was scheduled to start, almost all of the seats were taken.

"This is quite the gathering," Maggie noted.

Jesse shrugged. "Folks around here will take their entertainment any way they can get it."

"Or maybe they appreciate the time and effort that the teachers and students put into the productions."

"Maybe," he allowed, guiding her closer to the front, where his sister and the rest of the family were sitting.

Looking around as they made their way down the center aisle between the rows of seats, Maggie was surprised by how many familiar faces were in the crowd.

Caleb Dalton was there with his fiancée, Mallory Franklin, whose niece Lily was singing in the choir and one of the angels in the pageant. In addition, Maggie recognized several members of the Rust Creek Falls Newcomers Club, including Vanessa Brent—recently engaged to Jonah Traub—Jordyn Leigh Cates and Julie Smith. She knew some of their stories—Lily Franklin had played a big role in bringing her aunt and the boss's son together; Vanessa had met Jonah while they were both working onsite at the soon-to-be-completed Maverick Manor—and that some of the others were still looking to lasso the cowboy of their dreams.

She also knew that several of the single newcomers probably envied her the attention of the handsome cowboy she'd married. But while she might have Jesse's ring on her finger, she didn't have the one thing she really wanted: his heart.

Although she was undoubtedly a newcomer, too, she'd married Jesse so quickly after moving to Rust Creek Falls that a lot of people viewed her as his wife first, forgetting that she was also a transplant. Which was funny, because Jesse never did. In fact, she didn't think a single day had gone by since they'd married that he hadn't made at least one passing reference to the life she'd left behind in LA.

He wants you to stay, but he's afraid you won't.

Nina's words echoed in the back of her mind as Maggie took a seat beside her husband. In the row immediately in front of them was Jesse's sister with her husband. On the other side of Nina were her parents, and on the other side of Dallas were his. The Hatfields and the McCoys of Rust Creek Falls playing nice—or at least pretending to—for the sake of their children and grandchildren. Seeing them here together gave Maggie hope that the baby she was carrying might also succeed in bringing her and Jesse closer together.

As far as school plays went, Jesse decided it was entertaining. But not quite entertaining enough to keep his attention on the stage while he was seated beside his bride. He wasn't usually so easily distracted, but being close to Maggie made it impossible for him to focus on anything else.

With every breath he took, he breathed in the scent of her skin—something light and spicy. The scent was too subtle to be perfume, so he guessed it was probably some kind of lotion she rubbed on her body. A conclusion that tantalized his mind with the mental image of her delicate hands smoothing fragrant lotion over the bare, silky skin of her shoulders, her arms, her breasts...

The sound of applause jolted him back to the present. He automatically put his hands together as the kids on stage took a bow.

"There will now be a fifteen-minute intermission," the eighth-grade emcee announced. "Please help yourself to the cookies and hot drinks available outside."

The auditorium was suddenly filled with the sound of chair legs scraping against the floor as parents and grandparents and other guests hurried for the snacks.

"Do you want anything?" he asked Maggie.

She shook her head as she rose to her feet. "Just to stretch my legs."

He noticed that several older kids, not in costume, were on the stage now, pushing aside the long table that had been the setting of the Thanksgiving feast to set up a makeshift stable for the upcoming nativity scene.

"It's hard to believe that we're going to have a son or a daughter up on that stage someday," he said.

"Not for several years yet," Maggie pointed out to him.

"I know, but it started me thinking... Do you know if our baby is a boy or a girl?"

She shook her head. "Do you want to know?"

"I'm not sure," he admitted. "In some ways, I think it would make planning easier."

"We'd know whether to buy pink or blue burp cloths."

He smiled in response to her teasing. "There is that."

"I have an appointment for an ultrasound tomorrow. We should be able to find out the baby's gender, depending on his or her position." She hesitated a second, then said, "I know it's short notice, but you could come with me, if you want."

"I'd like that," he immediately replied.

"I should have asked you before, but you've been so busy…" Her explanation trailed off.

Yes, he'd been busy making himself busy, and he suspected that she knew it. But he still couldn't admit it to her now, because that would also require admitting that he didn't know how to be the husband she wanted—the husband he wanted to be to her.

Before he could manufacture an appropriate reply, Tara Jones—the third-grade teacher—stopped beside them.

"Mr. and Mrs. Crawford—how wonderful to see you here tonight."

Although her greeting encompassed both of them, she seemed to be speaking to Maggie, making Jesse suspect that she was a client. Her next words dispelled that theory.

"I know I said it before—but I have to thank you again for all of your help with the costumes and props."

"I really didn't do very much," Maggie said.

"We would never have had everything ready on time without you," Tara insisted. Then she turned to Jesse. "In case your wife didn't tell you, she made thirty pilgrim hats and an equal number of native headbands, painted the starry sky for the nativity scene and designed the wings and halos for the angels."

"You might want to save your thanks until after the pageant, in case the sky falls down."

Tara chuckled. "It's not going to fall down. And even if it did, it wouldn't matter. What matters is that you gave us the extra hands we desperately needed to get everything done in time for tonight."

Maggie smiled. "And that the kids all seem to be having a good time."

"They definitely are," the teacher agreed. "And now I'm going backstage to make sure their costumes are on before we continue the show."

Jesse waited until she was out of earshot before he turned to his wife. "I didn't know you'd helped out with this."

"I put in a few hours when I had nothing to do at the office," Maggie admitted, settling into her chair again as the other audience members began to return to their seats.

"It sounds like you put in more than a few hours."

She shrugged. "I had time on my hands."

He impulsively reached for one of those hands—it was small and soft in comparison to his, but for all of its delicacy, it was also strong. Not unlike Maggie herself.

She was a California girl experiencing a Montana winter, and he wondered if it was only her first or also her last. If she made it through the season, would she stay through the spring and the summer? How long would she last so far away from the bright lights of the big city? And how long did she need to stay before he stopped anticipating that she'd pack her bags and hightail it back to LA?

Right now, she seemed happy enough, and he hadn't been doing anything to make her happy. He'd been leaving her to her own devices, certain she would get bored and be gone. Maybe he was pushing her away, or at least testing her steadfastness. And yeah, it had only been a couple of weeks, but so far, she'd stuck. Which got him to thinking... What if he actually let her know that he wanted her to stay? What if he made an effort to make her want to stay?

There was a connection between them—he'd felt it from the first. It was real and strong. She made him want to open up to her in a way that he hadn't opened up to a woman in a long time, to share not just his home but his life and his heart, and that was more than a little scary.

Watching her watch the kids onstage, he let himself consider the possibilities. Maybe she could grow to love Montana—and him—enough to want to stay. Maybe they really could raise this child—and other children—together.

But there was still a part of him that was afraid to let himself believe, certain that as soon as he started to plan for their future together, she'd knock him down and stomp on his heart.

Don't make Maggie pay for what Shaelyn did to you.

Nina's words echoed in the back of his mind.

He knew that most of his family had had concerns when he'd told them that he and Maggie were getting married—and why. And although only ten days had passed since the wedding, Nina had become her new sister-in-law's biggest cheerleader.

But not her only supporter. Ben Dalton had nothing but praise for the young attorney he'd taken on. And even Sutter had mentioned how appreciative Paige was of Maggie's work at the law office, because it freed her father up to spend more time with his family.

Obviously their faith was well-placed. She was willing to tackle whatever legal issues were assigned to her, she was studying for her exams, and even outside her area of expertise she'd stepped in to help where help was needed. She was making an effort to fit in, to be accepted by the community, and the residents of Rust Creek Falls were starting to give her a chance—which, he realized, was more than he'd done.

Even while she'd been reciting her vows, he'd been holding his breath, waiting for her to announce that she'd changed her mind.

But despite his best efforts, he'd got used to having her around. He looked forward to seeing her at the breakfast table in the morning and having dinner with her every night. He enjoyed talking to her about his day and hers, and he enjoyed the silence when they didn't feel like talking. He felt comfortable around her—except when being in close proximity to her was decidedly *un*comfortable because she tempted him to want more, to believe they could have more.

They were connected by their baby and their marriage. But he'd meant it when he'd told her he wasn't looking for love, and he knew that he needed to maintain some kind of boundaries between them if he was going to protect his heart. He was already sharing his name, his house and almost every part of his life. If he shared his bed, there would be no more boundaries between them, nothing to prevent him from falling the rest of the way in love with her.

It was that certainty that prevented him from giving in to the ever-growing desire he felt for her.

At least for now.

Maggie had been referred to Dr. Gaynor in Kalispell by her ob-gyn in Los Angeles, and the first time she met her, she was impressed by the doctor's warmth, compassion and efficiency. Dr. Gaynor didn't believe in overbooking her patients, which meant that while emergencies did occasionally arise, it was unusual for there to be more than one or two women in the waiting room.

So it didn't surprise her that she was taken into an exam room at 10:59 a.m. for her eleven o'clock appointment, or that the doctor entered the room only three minutes later.

It did surprise her when the doctor said to Jesse, "You must be the husband."

He nodded and offered his hand. "Jesse Crawford."

"Susan Gaynor." She must have noticed Maggie's surprise, because she smiled. "The last time I saw you, you said that you might be getting married," the doctor reminded Maggie. "This time, you came with a man and a ring on your finger."

"We got married on the fifteenth," Maggie confirmed.

"Congratulations," Dr. Gaynor said to both of them. "And thank you—" her gaze shifted to Jesse "—for taking the time to come here today. It's always nice to see a husband supporting his wife through her pregnancy."

"I'm happy to be here," he said sincerely. "And to do anything I can to help Maggie over the next five months."

"The next five months are the easy part," the doctor teased. "The real challenges—and joys—come with the baby."

Jesse reached for her hand, linked their fingers together. "We're looking forward to both."

"Good answer," Dr. Gaynor said. "And I'm happy to report that everything looks great with both your wife and the baby. In fact—" she turned to Maggie now "—you've gained two pounds since I last saw you."

"I knew I shouldn't have eaten those Christmas cookies that Nina sent home with us last night," the mom-to-be grumbled.

The doctor chuckled. "A special treat every once in a while isn't going to hurt you or your baby so long as you're also eating lots of fruits, vegetables, whole grains and proteins."

"I'm eating lots of everything," Maggie confirmed.

"Good. That first trimester weight loss could have been problematic, but it's apparent that you've been taking good care of yourself and your baby.

"Have you felt any movement?"

"I don't think so," Maggie said, her grip on his hand instinctively tightening.

"It's nothing to be concerned about," the doctor assured her. "A lot of first-time moms don't recognize the little flutters as fetal movement. If you haven't noticed anything yet, you will soon enough."

Dr. Gaynor's glance shifted from Maggie to Jesse and back again. "Do either of you have any questions at this stage?"

He looked at Maggie, who shook her head.

The doctor followed the silent exchange, then directed her next comment to him. "A lot of first-time fathers worry about sex."

"Nope," he said quickly, vehemently. "No worries there."

"Good." The doctor nodded, but she didn't leave it at that. "But just in case you were wondering, there are absolutely no restrictions on intercourse right up to the day of delivery, so long as Maggie's comfortable and there aren't any complications in her pregnancy."

"Okay…um…yep. That's great."

Maggie didn't know if Jesse was looking at her, because she didn't dare look at him. Obviously they'd had sex—she wouldn't be here otherwise. But the doctor couldn't know, thankfully, that they hadn't been intimate for some time. In fact, for reasons she didn't understand and that her husband hadn't bothered to share with her, they hadn't even consummated their marriage.

Not that she was going to discuss that with him in the doctor's office—or anywhere else, apparently. Because although it was a question that continued to keep her awake at night, she wasn't entirely sure she wanted to know his answer. She didn't want to hear him confirm that he didn't want her—he only wanted their baby.

But she couldn't help wondering when and why he'd stopped wanting her. When they'd made love the first time after she'd told him that she was pregnant, he'd seemed captivated by the subtle changes in her body, awed by the realization that there was a tiny life growing inside of her.

Of course, with each day that passed, that tiny life was getting a little bit bigger. And although she'd only gained two pounds since that day, she was barely able to fasten the button on her pants now, which meant that she was going to have to start wearing maternity clothes soon. And if Jesse found her barely noticeable baby bump unappealing, how was he going to feel in a few more months?

"Are you ready to have a look at that baby of yours now?" Dr. Gaynor's question interrupted her musing.

It was only when Jesse squeezed her hand that Maggie realized he was still holding it—had been holding it almost from the minute they walked into the doctor's office.

She nodded in response to the doctor's inquiry.

"I'll send the technician in."

The technician, who introduced herself as Carla, wheeled in a cart with the ultrasound machine on it. It only took her a minute to set up, then she asked the mom-to-be to lift her shirt.

Maggie's pregnancy wasn't yet obvious—at least not to Jesse and not in the clothes she usually wore. In fact, she did such a good job of hiding any evidence of her pregnancy that he sometimes almost forgot she was pregnant— except he knew that she would never have chosen to move to Rust Creek Falls and marry him if not for their baby. He suspected the loose-fitting tops were a deliberate choice, to postpone the inevitable gossip and speculation that would run rampant when her condition became public knowledge. While he understood her reasons, he wanted to shout the news of her pregnancy from the rooftops for all of the world to hear. But because she'd done such a good job disguising her baby bump, he was surprised when she lifted the hem of her tunic-style top and he saw that there was an undeniable roundness to her belly.

The technician squirted gel onto the exposed skin and pressed a probe to her belly. A rhythmic whooshing sound filled the silence and the fuzzy display on the monitor screen began to take shape.

"Oh. Wow."

Jesse felt stunned—and humbled—as he registered the shape of their baby: the outline of the head and the body, even the skinny little legs and arms, and—most awesome and overwhelming—the rapid beating of the heart inside the chest.

He had some experience with ultrasounds—mostly with respect to equine fetuses. But this was completely outside his realm of experience. This was an actual human baby— his and Maggie's baby. He knew that he'd done very little to help grow this miracle inside of her. Yes, he'd contributed half of the baby's DNA, but since then, he'd done nothing. She was the one who was giving their baby everything he or she needed, the only one who could.

He wanted to say something to express the awe and gratitude that filled his heart, but his throat was suddenly tight, so he settled for squeezing Maggie's hand.

"Your baby is almost eight inches long and weighs about fourteen ounces," Carla told them. "Completely within normal range for twenty-one weeks."

"I've gained eight pounds and less than one of that is the baby?"

"Which is completely normal," the technician said patiently. "Now that I'm finished with all the measurements, do you want to know your baby's gender?"

Maggie looked at Jesse. They'd talked about the possibility but hadn't made a final decision, and he was grateful that she was asking for his input now. He considered, wavered, then nodded.

"Can you tell?" Maggie asked.

"I can tell," Carla said. "But I never do unless the parents want to know."

"We want to know," she decided.

The technician smiled. "It's a girl."

A girl.

Maggie honestly hadn't thought she had any preference, but she would have guessed that Jesse wanted a boy. But when she looked at him now, trying to gauge his reaction to the news, he didn't look disappointed. In fact, he was smiling like the proud father he would be in another few months.

"Were you hoping for a boy?" she asked softly.

He immediately shook his head. "My only hope is that both you and the baby are healthy."

The sincerity in his tone assured Maggie that he meant it. And the way he was looking at her—with warmth and affection—gave her hope that sharing the experience of "seeing" their baby for the first time together might bring them closer.

The technician gave her a paper towel to wipe the gel off her belly, and the moment was broken.

"Do you feel up to making another stop before we head back home?" Jesse asked when they left the doctor's office.

"Does that stop include lunch?"

He chuckled. "That stop can definitely include lunch," he promised. "What do you want to eat?"

"A burger," she answered without hesitation.

"Then we'll get you a burger."

Chapter Fourteen

They found a diner around the corner from the medical center. It was an old-fashioned-style eatery with Formica tabletops and red vinyl benches and stools lined up at the counter. The menu was quite extensive, offering more than a dozen different types of burgers with countless toppings, French fries, sweet potato fries, onion rings, coleslaw or green salad, and milk shakes and ice-cream floats.

Maggie ordered a bacon cheeseburger and a side salad, then picked at the fries on Jesse's plate. Not that he minded—it was all he could do to finish the spicy barbecue chicken sandwich on sourdough bread that he'd ordered—but he was curious.

"If you wanted fries, why didn't you just order fries?" he finally asked.

"Because the salad is healthier."

"But you're eating fries, anyway."

"Only a few," she said defensively. "And only after I ate my veggies."

He nudged his plate closer to her. "I don't mind sharing," he assured her. "I was just wondering about your rationale."

"I never even used to like French fries all that much," she said. "But lately, I can't seem to get enough."

"Any other unusual food cravings?"

"Red meat," she said.

"I noticed we've been eating a lot of beef."

Her gaze tracked the slice of apple pie that a waitress carried past their table to deliver to another customer.

"And apple pie?" he prompted.

She turned her attention back to him. "Sorry?"

He smiled. "Do you want dessert?"

"I probably shouldn't."

"Which doesn't actually answer the question," he said.

"I'm not sure if I want dessert or if that pie just looked really good."

"Should I get a slice of pie and ask for two forks?"

"Only if you want pie," she said. "With ice cream."

So he ordered the apple pie with ice cream and two forks.

After it was delivered, he watched her fork slide through the flaky crust and layers of sweet, sticky apple slices. Her lips closed around the tines of the fork, her eyes drifted shut and she let out a sigh of pure pleasure that stirred an appetite inside him that had nothing to do with dessert.

She chewed slowly, savoring the flavor, and finally swallowed.

"You have to try this," she told him.

"I ordered it for you."

She shook her head. "I'd feel way too guilty if I ate the whole thing myself."

So he picked up the second fork and took a bite.

There was something intimate about sharing a dessert. Maybe it went back to the communal consumption of ancient times, when a hunter shared his catch with his mate and their children, proof of their relationship to one another. Or maybe it was that watching Maggie eat was an incredibly erotic experience.

The pie was good, but he much preferred letting Maggie savor it.

Her tongue swept over her bottom lip, licking away the smear of ice cream. He knew that her lips were even sweeter than ice cream, and he had an almost insatiable desire to lean across the table and sample her flavor. It seemed as if it had been years since he'd kissed her, rather than the ten days that had passed since their wedding. But it wasn't easy holding his want of her in check, and he knew that if he gave in to the urge to kiss her, he wouldn't be able to stop with one kiss.

"I'm glad you're enjoying your dessert," he said.

"It's always a treat to eat something that someone else has prepared."

"And I haven't taken you out to eat anywhere since we got married," he realized. Equally startling was the realization that he hadn't taken her out at all *before* they were married. They had gone out for dinner in LA, and although he'd insisted on paying the bill, she'd chosen the restaurant, so he didn't figure he should get credit for that.

"We're going to your parents' house for Thanksgiving."

"That hardly counts."

She shrugged. "I don't need to be taken out or entertained."

And maybe it was because she didn't that he found himself wanting to make the effort. "I haven't been a very attentive husband," he acknowledged. "My only excuse is that I don't have a lot of experience with this kind of thing."

"It's my first marriage, too," she said lightly.

"I meant…dating and other courtship rituals."

"I'm your wife, Jesse. You don't have to court me."

"I should have courted you properly before we were married."

"I guess we did things a little out of order," she agreed. "But I'm not sorry, because they got us to where we are now."

"You don't miss LA?"

"Only my family," she told him. Then she gave him a half smile. "And the weather."

"The weather can be a challenge, even for those who were born and bred in Montana," he admitted.

"I asked Lissa how she survived her first winter in Rust Creek Falls—she said she wouldn't have survived at all if she hadn't had Gage to snuggle up to every night."

"I don't think I like the idea of you snuggling up to your cousin's husband," he teased.

"I don't think Lissa would, either," she admitted.

And although she smiled, her gaze shifted away, as if she was disappointed by his response. Which made him wonder—had she been suggesting that she wanted to snuggle up to him?

Before he could decide whether or not to pursue the possibility, the waitress brought the bill to their table.

When Jesse asked if they could make a stop before heading back to Rust Creek Falls, she'd assumed it was to pick up something that he needed for the horses. So she was more than a little surprised when he pulled into the parking lot of a strip mall—and parked in front of a toy store.

He strode purposefully through the front doors, as if he'd been there before and knew exactly where he was going. Considering the way he doted on his eleven-month-old niece, she would bet he'd been there several times before. He guided her down the main aisle to a section titled Cuddly Critters that was lined with big cubes stacked floor to ceiling and filled with stuffed animals of various breeds, sizes and colors.

Jesse zeroed in on the pink teddy bears, rifled through the selection, then pulled one out and handed it to Maggie.

Her fingers sank into fur that was unbelievably soft and plush. The bear was the color of cotton candy, with skinny arms and legs ending in oversized paws. The head was big, too, with a slightly paler muzzle, a brown nose, and eyes and a half smile stitched onto the fabric. It was, without a doubt, the cutest baby teddy bear she'd ever seen, and when he put it in her arms, her heart just melted.

She looked up at him. "For our baby?"

He shook his head. "For you. To remember the day that we found out about our baby girl."

"I have a very old pink teddy bear that sits on my bedside table at home," she said wistfully.

"I saw it when I was there," he admitted.

"My parents gave it to me the day I was adopted."

"I guess teddy bears are a pretty common theme."

But there was nothing commonplace about his gesture, and tears filled her eyes as she impulsively hugged him, squishing the bear between them. "Thank you."

"I should be thanking you," he said gruffly. "You're giving me the greatest gift of all in our baby, and I don't know how to tell you how grateful I am. Looking at our daughter on the ultrasound monitor, I realized how different things might have been…if you'd chosen not to tell me…or if you'd decided to give her away."

"I wouldn't have," she promised him. "It might have taken me a while to share the news, but I would never have kept it from you."

He brushed a strand of hair off her cheek, tucked it behind her ear. His deep blue eyes reflected so much of what he was feeling: affection, warmth—want?

Her breath caught in her throat as she thought, for one brief moment, that he was actually going to kiss her. She didn't care if they were standing in the middle of a toy store, she wanted to feel his lips on hers. It had been so long since he'd kissed her, too long.

But instead of lowering his head toward her, he took a step back, away from temptation. Or maybe she was the only one who was tempted.

She'd seen the surprise on his face when she lifted her shirt and he realized the tiny curve of her belly was bigger and rounder since the last time he'd seen her naked. And although she was still on the small side for twenty-one weeks, there was no longer any denying that she was pregnant. The body that he'd so thoroughly explored with his hands and his lips back in the summer was growing and changing—her subtle curves weren't nearly as subtle anymore, and his desire for her wasn't nearly as palpable.

She sat with the teddy bear in her lap throughout the drive home and consoled herself with the knowledge that at least now she'd have something to cuddle up with at night.

It wasn't what—or rather who—she wanted to be with, but the company of a plush bear was better than nothing…

Maggie went into the office for a couple of hours after she and Jesse returned from Kalispell. He, predictably, went to Traub Stables and warned her that he wouldn't be home until late. When the phone rang around nine o'clock that night, she thought it might be him calling to tell her that he was on his way home. She was only a little disappointed when she heard her mother's voice on the other end of the line.

"I just called to see how you're doing," Christa said when her daughter answered. "You had a doctor's appointment today, didn't you?"

Maggie had to smile. "You're twelve hundred miles away, in the middle of discoveries for a multimillion-dollar class action lawsuit, and you remembered the date of my doctor's appointment?"

"Of course," her mother said simply.

"Everything's fine," Maggie told her. "The baby is healthy and growing."

"And the baby's mom?"

"She's fine, too. In fact, I've gained back almost all of the weight I lost in the first trimester."

"That's good."

"I think I'm going to wear that Isabella Oliver wrap maternity dress that you sent to me for Thanksgiving." She didn't tell her mother that she'd also be wearing faux fur–lined knee-high boots and a down coat, because she did not want to hear about the balmy weather in SoCal.

"Maybe you could make a quick weekend trip this way sometime soon for us to do some more shopping," Christa suggested. "For you and for the baby."

"I'd like that," Maggie agreed.

"I wish you could be here for Thanksgiving," Christa said. "Both you and Jesse, I mean."

She was glad for the distance that separated them, so her mother couldn't see the tears that stung her eyes. "We'll make the trip for Christmas," she promised.

"Christmas still seems so far away."

"It will be here before we know it."

"So what are your plans for this holiday?"

"We're having a big meal with Jesse's family—all fifteen of them."

Christa laughed. "That should be an experience."

"No doubt."

"How's the new job?"

"Good," Maggie said. "Different, but good. I'm doing a little bit of everything, but not a lot of anything."

"I'm sure you don't miss working sixty hours a week for Brian Nash."

"No," she agreed. "I feel a little bit like I'm at loose ends right now, but I know I'll be glad for the slower pace when the baby comes."

They chatted a little more, about the class action suit, a new movie star client—unnamed to protect the solicitor-client privilege—who had hired Gavin to fight a paternity claim, and the new woman—a Laker girl—that Ryan was dating.

"Are you sure everything is okay?" Christa asked when their conversation had finally wound down. "Because LA might seem like a long way from Rust Creek Falls, but if you need anything at all, you just say the word and I'll be there."

Maggie was glad that her mother couldn't see the tears that filled her eyes. "Thanks, Mom. But everything's fine."

"You don't sound fine."

"I guess I'm just missing you and Dad. I've never not been home for Thanksgiving."

"You don't feel like Rust Creek Falls is your home now?" her mother asked gently.

"No, I do," Maggie hastened to assure her, again grateful that her mother couldn't see her face because Christa always could tell when any of her kids was being less than honest. "Like I said—I'm just missing you and Dad. Even Ryan."

That made her mother chuckle. "Happy Thanksgiving, Maggie."

"You, too, Mom."

Maggie was putting her boots on when Jesse came in from his final check on the animals Wednesday night.

"Going somewhere?" he asked.

"To the grocery store."

Because she'd specified *grocery*, he knew she didn't mean Crawford's. "We were just in Kalispell yesterday for your doctor's appointment," he reminded her.

"I know," she admitted. "But I wasn't thinking about Thanksgiving then."

"And you're thinking about Thanksgiving now?"

"Because it's tomorrow," she reminded him. "And I can't show up at your parents' house empty-handed."

"My mom's been doing Thanksgiving dinner for more years than I've been alive," Jesse pointed out. "I assure you, everything is covered."

"I want to make something," she insisted.

He sighed. "It's late and it's already been a long day."

"I don't expect you to go with me—I just thought you might want to know where I was going."

"Is Lissa going with you?"

"No."

He frowned. "You're going by yourself?"

"I know the way," she assured him.

"But it's late," he said again.

"It's not quite seven-thirty and the store's open until nine."

She made the statement matter-of-factly, as if she was perfectly capable of driving twenty minutes to an out-of-town grocery store to pick up a few items. And, of course, she was—he was just taken aback by her independence.

He'd lost count of the number of times he'd suggested to Shaelyn that she should go into Kalispell to go shopping or to a movie or even just to get one of those fancy over-priced iced coffee drinks that she liked and that couldn't be found in Rust Creek Falls.

But she never wanted to go anywhere without him. And she had a knack for making him feel guilty for even suggesting she should be on her own for half an hour when he'd been away from her for most of the day. And what if something happened when she was driving *all the way* to and from Kalispell?

As if he needed any further proof that Maggie was nothing like Shaelyn, she already had her boots and coat on and her keys in hand.

"Wait."

She paused at the door. "Did you want something from the store?"

"I want to go with you," he decided.

"That's really not necessary."

And he knew it was true. She didn't need him to go to the grocery store with her. In fact, she didn't seem to need him for much of anything. There wasn't anything she couldn't do on her own—including having and raising a child.

Which supported what Nina had said—that Maggie wasn't with him because she needed him but because she wanted to be with him.

And he realized that he didn't like the idea of her driving to Kalispell on her own. Not because he was worried about anything that might happen, just because he wanted to be with her.

"I know," he finally said. "But I'd like to come, anyway."

She looked at him for a moment, then turned back to the door. "Then let's go."

Maggie was undeniably apprehensive about spending Thanksgiving with Jesse's family. Partly because the last time she'd been invited to Todd and Laura's house, she'd abruptly—and rudely—dropped the bombshell about her pregnancy on them, and partly because this was the first time since the wedding that she'd be in the same room with all of Jesse's siblings—and the first time she'd see most of them since her husband had shared the news about their baby.

"What have you got there?" Laura asked, gesturing to the covered bowls in each of Jesse's and Maggie's hands.

"This one's coleslaw," she said, holding it up. "And Jesse's got the mac and cheese carbonara."

"Mac and cheese *what*?" Todd asked.

"It's got bacon in it," Jesse said, knowing that was his father's weakness.

"Well, I'll have to try that," he decided.

"You didn't have to bring anything," her mother-in-law protested.

"It's a lot of work to make a meal for so many people," Maggie acknowledged. "I wanted to at least make a small contribution."

"Well, that was real thoughtful," Laura said, basking a little in her new daughter-in-law's compliment. Then she gestured for them to join the rest of the family in the living room. "Come in, come in. We'll be putting dinner on the table shortly."

"Can I give you a hand with anything?" Maggie offered.

Her mother-in-law shook her head. "We've got everything covered. Oh—except that we do need one more place set at the table."

"I'm doing it now," Callie said from the dining room.

"One more?" Jesse queried.

Laura nodded to her husband. "Ask your father."

His father shrugged. "When I stopped by the store to pick up a pint of ice cream, I saw Homer Gilmore wandering the street. Since I knew we'd have more than enough food to feed the army reserves, I asked him to join us for the meal."

"That was…generous," Jesse noted.

And, Maggie could tell by his tone, unexpected.

"Everybody sit," Laura directed, as Nina and Natalie began to set bowls and platters of food around the table. "Justin—you can pour the wine. Brad—get Noelle's high chair from the kitchen. Jesse—you make sure everyone finds a seat. Nate—you come get the turkey."

Justin made his way around the table, pouring the wine. "Oops—forgot about the bun in the oven," he said, lifting the bottle away from Maggie's glass.

"Gramma took the buns out of the oven," seven-year-old Robbie said, pointing to the basket on the table.

"Yes, I did," Laura confirmed, sending a narrow-eyed look in her son's direction.

"What would you like to drink?" Natalie asked Maggie.

"Water's fine," she replied, because glasses of that were already set around the table along with a pitcher for refills.

When everyone was settled, Todd said grace, expressing thanks for the bountiful feast on the table and the gathering of family and friends. Then the bowls and platters were passed around, and people chatted easily as they filled their plates.

Laura Crawford had indeed prepared enough food to feed an army—or at least the army reserves—confirming Jesse's assertion that Maggie's contribution was unnecessary. But she was pleased to note that Dallas's three sons all wanted to try her mac and cheese.

"What's that?" Brad asked, warily eyeing the bowl that Jesse offered to him.

"It's coleslaw."

Brad scowled as he looked more closely at the salad. "But it's got raisins…and nuts."

"And it's delicious," Natalie said.

"Did you make this?" Brad asked his youngest sister.

"Maggie did."

"Oh." He glanced apologetically at his new sister-in-law. "I usually eat my fruit after dinner, inside a pie crust."

"He says as he spoons cranberry sauce onto his plate," Nina noted drily.

He scowled at that. "Cranberry sauce isn't fruit—it's a condiment."

"It's fruit," his mother informed him.

"Well, my plate's kind of full right now," Brad said, passing the bowl of coleslaw to Nate's fiancée, Callie, on his other side. "I'll try some on the next go-round."

"Can I have some more mac 'n' cheese?" Robbie asked, lifting his plate up.

"Eat some of your veggies and meat first," his father admonished.

"But I like the mac 'n' cheese best," the little boy said.

Which reassured Maggie that she'd at least made one good choice.

"What kind of cheese is in that sauce?" Laura asked.

"There are four different kinds," Maggie said. "Cheddar, Asiago, Fontina and Parmigiano Reggiano."

"Do we carry those in the store?" Laura asked her oldest daughter.

"Cheddar and Parmigiano," Nina said. "But even I go shopping in Kalispell to pick up items that we don't stock on a regular basis."

And all three of Dallas's boys were devouring the mac and cheese carbonara as if they'd never tasted anything so good.

Jesse slid an arm across her shoulders. "Better than the stuff that comes out of a box, that's for sure."

"You haven't tried the coleslaw."

"Fruit and nuts are for dessert," he echoed his brother.

"And I can say that because I don't eat cranberry sauce, either."

Across the table, Justin was drowning his mashed potatoes in gravy as he spoke to Nate. "How is construction of the resort coming along?"

Other conversations quieted as everyone wanted to hear the details. Maggie had been surprised to learn that, only a few months earlier, Nate had been thinking about leaving Rust Creek Falls. Instead, he'd decided to buy a piece of local property to open a resort, similar to what was in Thunder Canyon. Work had progressed steadily, and Maverick Manor was scheduled for a Christmas Eve grand opening.

"Is there going to be a honeymoon suite?" Nina asked.

"You've already had a honeymoon," her oldest brother reminded her.

"But Jesse and Maggie haven't," she pointed out.

"There is a honeymoon suite," Callie confirmed. "On the top floor, of course, with a gas fireplace in the lounge area and a jetted tub big enough for two in the bath."

"It sounds impressive," Maggie said, because Callie seemed to expect her to say something.

"Let us know when you've got a couple of days free and I'll reserve it for you," Nate promised.

Jesse looked at his wife. "What do you think?"

She was tempted to ask Nate if the room had two beds, because she didn't think Jesse would be willing to go if they actually had to sleep under the same covers.

"That's a generous offer," she said instead. "But we're going to be in Los Angeles for Christmas this year."

Which would present them with the same dilemma under a different roof. As close as Maggie was to her parents, she didn't want to explain to them that she wasn't sharing a bed with her husband. So they were going to have to share a bed—or one of them would have to sleep on the floor, and it wasn't going to be her.

But they had several weeks before they had to worry about that. Right now, she was focused on getting through this holiday with Jesse's family.

She was grateful that his siblings seemed to have accepted her. His parents were still lukewarm, and she didn't really blame them. They didn't know her well enough to know that she hadn't set out to trap their son.

On the other hand, her parents didn't know Jesse very well, either, but they didn't blame him for the situation. Maybe because they at least knew her well enough to know that she wouldn't be here now if she didn't want to be. Baby or no baby, she wouldn't have married him if she didn't love him. She wondered if Jesse was ever going to figure out the same thing.

"How about New Year's Eve?" Nate suggested now. "We've taken a few reservations for December 31 already, but the honeymoon suite is still available."

"I promise you'll love it," Callie said to Maggie. "The painting's done and the window coverings are going to be installed this week. Then it's just the finishing touches— bedding, towels, decorations, et cetera. If you get a chance, you should stop by for an informal tour."

Maggie appreciated the overture. "I'd like that—thanks."

"I'll pencil you in for New Year's Eve, then," Nate decided.

To which Homer responded, "We must rescue the child."

Maggie looked at Jesse, not sure if the old man was referring to their unborn child or Noelle or one of Dallas's sons. The old man didn't appear to be looking at anyone in particular but was staring at his plate and shaking his head. "We must save the child."

"Why's he saying that?" Robbie asked Nina.

"I have no idea," she admitted to her youngest stepson.

"He's creepy," Ryder muttered.

Thankfully the boy was far enough away from Homer that the old man couldn't hear him. And, truthfully, Maggie couldn't help but agree, at least with respect to his behavior today.

"Who wants pie?" Laura asked brightly.

"I think we're going to skip dessert and get the kids home," Nina told her mother.

The family matriarch looked as if she wanted to protest, then she glanced at Homer again and finally nodded. "I'll get you some pie to take with you."

Nina and Dallas ushered the kids away from the table, and Homer turned his attention to Maggie.

"We must rescue the child," he told her, his tone imploring.

While his eyes were on her, his gaze was unfocused, and she realized he wasn't looking at her so much as past her.

Were his strange prognostications merely the ramblings of a crazy old man—or were his words intended as some kind of warning to her? Was it possible that the child he was referring to was her own? And if so, why did he think her child needed to be saved?

Chapter Fifteen

"I think we should invite Homer Gilmore to the table every time we have dinner with your parents," Maggie said to Jesse when they got home that evening.

"Why is that?" her husband asked, sounding amused.

"Because his sporadic outbursts meant that people were staring at him instead of me every once in a while."

"Was it that bad?"

She shrugged.

"Well, you survived your first Crawford family Thanksgiving relatively unscathed."

"Pun intended?"

He just grinned.

"Since it's a day to count our blessings, I'll say that your mother is a fabulous cook."

"And she always makes sure there's enough so that everyone has some leftovers to take home."

"She even packed a turkey sandwich for Homer Gilmore before your dad took him back to town."

"Did he freak you out?"

"Homer or your dad?"

Her husband chuckled. "Homer."

She shrugged again. "Not really. Although sometimes, the way he looked at me when he talked about saving the baby, I wondered if he was talking about our baby."

"I don't think even he knew what he was talking about," Jesse said. "He's just a crazy old man."

"Maybe," she allowed. "But he seemed sincerely worried. Does he have any children?"

"I have no idea. He's not originally from around here. And while it's hard to imagine him in a relationship with anyone, I suppose it's possible."

"I just wish there was something I could do to help him."

"Maybe you should keep your distance from him."

"He's not dangerous."

"Probably not," Jesse agreed. "But I'd rather you didn't take any chances."

"I wouldn't do anything to risk our baby," she assured him.

"I'm not just worried about the baby."

She looked up at him, obviously surprised by his statement.

"Don't you realize how much I care about you, too?"

Care. There it was—a four-letter word that described his feelings for her. Unfortunately, it wasn't the four-letter word she'd been hoping to hear.

"Well, I'm not going to let anything happen to me or our baby," she said lightly.

He nodded. "Good. Now, how about a turkey sandwich?"

She shook her head. "I can't believe you're hungry again already."

"Turkey sandwiches are a Thanksgiving evening tradition."

"Not for me," she told him. "I couldn't eat another bite."

"How about pie?"

She started to shake her head again, paused. "Pumpkin?"

He chuckled. "We've got apple and pumpkin."

"Maybe just a sliver," she allowed, and followed him to the kitchen.

"Sit," he said, pointing to the breakfast bar. "I'll get it for you."

She sat. He cut a slice of the pie his mother had sent home, slid it onto a plate, added a fork and set it on the counter in front of her.

"I said a sliver," she reminded him.

"You're eating for two."

Actually, her doctor had warned her that was a fallacy, but considering the fact that her weight wasn't an issue—not yet, anyway—she picked up the fork and dug into the pie without further comment.

"I wish we had some of that mac and cheese left over," he said. "I barely got to sample it."

"It was a hit with the kids," she agreed.

"Not just the kids—even Brad had two helpings."

"But he wouldn't try the coleslaw."

Jesse just shrugged and washed down his sandwich with a tall glass of milk.

She expected him to push away from the table and escape to the barn with the excuse of one chore or another. Sure enough, he slid back his chair and stood up to clear away both of their plates, but then he surprised her by asking, "Do you want to watch some of the football game with me?"

She shook her head. "It's been a long day and I'm ready for bed."

"Are you feeling okay? You didn't overdo it, did you?"

"I'm fine," she assured him. "Just…tired."

And she was—not just physically, but emotionally. She was tired of wanting what she knew she couldn't have, tired of pretending that their marriage was something it wasn't, tired of hoping that he might one day love her the same way that she loved him.

It was her own fault. He'd told her from the beginning that he didn't want to fall in love—he just wanted their baby to have two parents.

It had seemed like a reasonable request at the time, but after almost two weeks of living together, so close and yet with so much distance between them, she realized this was going to be more difficult than she'd anticipated. Not just difficult, but painful, and she wasn't sure that she could continue like this for much longer.

They'd been married for twelve days and living like roommates. She thought they'd made some progress today. They'd spent several hours together, shared some quiet moments and comfortable silences. And he'd admitted that he cared about her. True, it was a long way from caring to loving, but she had to believe it was a step in the right direction.

Maybe she should stay up with him, at least for a little while. But being near Jesse wreaked havoc on her mind and her heart. What she really needed was distance— some time away from him to figure out what she really wanted and needed.

"I talked to my mom yesterday," she told him. "She invited me to LA for a shopping trip. Well, the invitation was to both of us, but I don't imagine that would be your idea of fun."

"It's not," he agreed. "And it seems a long way to go to do some shopping."

"Aside from the fact that I'd also get to spend some time with my parents, there are some fabulous baby stores in SoCal."

"Rust Creek Falls might not be a shopping mecca," he acknowledged, "but it has other advantages."

"I wasn't making a comparison."

But obviously he thought that she was, because he said, "I just wanted to remind you that this is a great place to raise a child.

"That's why I'm here," she reminded him. "So that we can raise our child in Rust Creek Falls, together."

"You're sure this is where you want to be?"

"This is exactly where I want to be," she said, wanting to reassure him. But then she realized that while it was true, it wasn't the whole truth. "Or *almost* where I want to be."

He frowned at the clarification. "Almost?"

She hesitated, doubts creeping in. Did she really want to go down this path without knowing where it might lead? But she decided that she did, because it beat the alternative of continuing to live the way they'd been living for almost two weeks. She hadn't married Jesse so they could live separate lives under the same roof.

She'd married him because she loved him and she wanted to be his wife in every sense of the word. But she didn't think he was quite ready for that heartfelt declaration just yet, so she only said, "I'd rather be in the bed across the hall from where I've been sleeping."

Across the hall was…his bed.

Jesse's gaze locked with hers, silently seeking—begging for—confirmation.

She didn't falter, didn't blink, and in the depths of her eyes he saw a reflection of the same desire that hummed in his veins. She wanted him—and he wanted her. He would be a fool to turn down what she was offering, and he never liked to be a fool.

But he realized now that he had been. Living in close proximity to Maggie since the wedding had been a delicious torture. She'd been close enough to touch, but he hadn't been certain she wanted his touch. He'd let himself be swayed by her brother's concern that she didn't know what she wanted instead of asking her what she wanted.

"I put your stuff in the other room because I didn't want to assume we'd share a bed just because we were married."

"I kind of hoped we'd share a bed because we wanted to," she told him. "If that is what you wanted."

"It's what I wanted—what I want," he confirmed. "I haven't stopped wanting you since the first day I saw you, and believe me, I've tried."

"Why?"

"Because I pushed you into marriage, and then it bothered me to think that you only married me because I pushed."

"If you knew me better, you'd know that nobody pushes me to do something I don't want to do."

"You wanted to marry me?"

She nodded. "I've never felt about anyone else the way I feel about you. And I've never experienced anything like the pleasure I've known in your arms."

In response to that, he lifted her into his arms and carried her to his bedroom.

He set her back on her feet beside the bed and lowered his mouth to hers. Her eyes drifted shut as her lips parted, welcoming a deeper kiss. Her tongue danced with his, a sensual rhythm that had his blood pounding in his veins, hot and demanding.

It took him a minute to figure out the wrap-style dress she was wearing. He thoroughly enjoyed running his hands over her torso, tracing her feminine curves in an effort to find the hidden zipper, but he really wanted to feel her bare skin beneath his palms. When he finally discovered the tie at her side—when she finally guided his searching hands to it—he nearly chuckled with giddy relief. With one quick tug, the knot loosened and the fabric parted. Then he was touching *her*, and the silky softness of her skin was even more tantalizing than he remembered.

He pushed the dress off her shoulders and let it fall to the floor, then he took a step back to look at her. She was wearing a pale pink bra, matching bikini panties and those thigh-high stockings that he'd always suspected were designed to drive a man to his knees. Literally.

He dropped to the floor in front of her, splayed his palms on her belly then slid them around to her back, pulling her closer to kiss her belly. Then his mouth moved lower to nuzzle the sweet heat between her thighs. Maggie sucked in a breath. He stroked her with his tongue, through the thin barrier of lace, and felt her thigh muscles quiver. He wanted her to tremble for him, but he didn't want her to sink to the floor.

He rose to his feet again and peeled away her bra, her panties, one stocking and the other. Then he eased her back onto the mattress and started to lower himself over her.

She lifted her hands, holding him away. "I want you naked, too," she told him.

He quickly stripped away his own clothes, then glanced at her with his brows raised. She answered his silent question with a smile and lifted her arms to embrace him.

He kissed her again, softly, sweetly. "You are so beautiful," he told her.

When Jesse looked at her the way he was looking at her right now, with warmth and affection in his gaze, Maggie felt beautiful. When he touched her the way he was touching her now, gently and reverently, she knew he saw her that way.

But if she was beautiful, he was breathtaking.

Maybe the life of a rancher wasn't as romantic as it was

depicted in the movies, but there wasn't any big-screen star who could hold a candle to Jesse Crawford. She let her hands roam over him, absorbing the smooth texture of bronzed skin stretched taut over all those glorious muscles, sculpted not in some Hollywood gym to look like a cowboy but through years of hard work actually *being* a cowboy.

She'd never known anyone like him, had never felt the way she felt with him, and the memory of what he had done—could do—to her body left her breathless and aching for him.

"Jesse…please."

"I will please you," he promised.

And he did. He made his way down her body, kissing and caressing every inch of her. Loving her with his mouth and his hands until everything inside of her twisted and tightened—and released.

He held her close—he was her anchor in the storm as endless waves of sensation washed over her. When those waves gradually subsided to ripples, he finally parted her thighs and buried himself in the wet heat between them, and the storm started all over again.

As they moved together in the thrillingly familiar rhythm of lovemaking, she felt connected to him in a way that was so much more than physical. And the way he looked at her, their gazes linked as tangibly as their bodies, she was sure that he must feel it, too.

Afterward, he held her tight against him, as if he couldn't bear to let her go. And she fell asleep listening to his heart beating, steady and strong, beneath her cheek and knew she was exactly where she wanted to be.

Maggie wasn't sure why she'd awakened—a quick glance at the clock on the bedside table confirmed that it was still early. Not surprisingly, Jesse was already up—and getting ready to walk out the door.

"Where are you going?"

"You're awake."

"After last night, I didn't expect to wake up alone." She sat up, tugging the sheet to cover her breasts.

"I got a message from Sutter."

"It's the day after Thanksgiving—a holiday for almost everyone in this country who doesn't work in retail."

"One of his friends has a yearling with some behavioral issues and he asked me to take a look at him," he said, as if that explained everything.

"And you have to go right now?"

"I told him I would."

And because Jesse was nothing if not a man of his word, she nodded. "When do you think you'll be back?"

"I don't really know."

It wasn't just the noncommittal response, it was the way his gaze kept shifting away, as if he couldn't bear to look at her, as if he was already out the door.

No—she wasn't going to jump to conclusions. They'd had a fabulous night together. She wasn't going to assume anything was wrong and sabotage the closeness they'd shared.

"Will you be home for lunch?"

"Probably."

But he didn't say that he'd keep her posted, and he didn't kiss her goodbye. He just said, "I'll see you later," and then he walked out the door.

She sat there for another minute, naked in his bed, staring at the empty doorway through which he'd disappeared and trying to make sense of what had just happened. But she couldn't, and tears welled up along with her frustration.

She didn't understand what was going on with him.

The night before, she'd felt so connected to him, not just physically but emotionally. She'd been certain that they'd turned a corner, that they were finally going to start living as husband and wife, building a life and preparing for the birth of their child together.

She'd expected to wake up in his arms; she'd even hoped they might make love again. She knew he had things to do around the ranch, that even on the day after Thanksgiving, stalls needed to be mucked out and animals fed, so she didn't expect he'd stay in bed with her all day. But she'd hoped he'd at least show *some* reluctance to leave her side.

Instead, he'd already been up and dressed and on his way out the door when she'd awakened. She wasn't just hurt by his disappearing act, she was baffled. Why was he so anxious to put distance between them? Did he really not have any feelings for her?

No, she didn't believe that. There was no way he could have kissed her and touched her and loved her the way he had unless he felt something. But she was tired of guessing the breadth and depth of those feelings. She couldn't keep doing this—she couldn't keep putting herself out there only to have him pull back every time they started to get close. She couldn't continue to live under the same roof with the man she loved if he didn't feel the same way.

She dried her tears and picked up the phone.

When the call connected at the other end, she took a deep breath and said, "Nina—I need to ask you a huge favor."

Jesse was more than halfway to Traub Stables before he finally acknowledged the question that had been hammering at his mind since he'd responded to Sutter's text: *What was he doing?*

Why had he walked away from the beautiful—and

naked—woman who was still in his bed? What was he afraid of?

Maggie wasn't Shaelyn. The woman he'd married wasn't anything like the girl he'd been engaged to for a short time so many years before. Maggie was smart and beautiful, warm and compassionate, sexy and fun. She was also making a real effort to meet people and make friends, to fit in—and she was succeeding. He'd heard nothing but positive comments from everyone who had got to know her, his brothers and sisters all liked her, and even his parents were starting to come around.

And most significant to Jesse, she'd left her job and her family in LA and moved to Rust Creek Falls so that they could raise their baby together. He'd been so grateful for that decision he hadn't really asked why. He hadn't dared let himself hope that she'd made the choices she had because she loved him—as he loved her.

And with sudden clarity, he realized that was exactly what he'd been afraid of.

They'd both agreed to this legal union in order to give their baby a family. He'd made it clear that he didn't want to fall in love. But apparently his heart hadn't got that memo, because that was exactly what had happened.

He should have known, from day one, that he was fighting a losing battle. Because he'd started falling the first day he met her—no, even before then. The first time he saw her.

Had he really thought he could share a life with her—his home, his bed—and keep his emotions out of it? If so, he was obviously a bigger fool than he thought.

He might not have wanted to fall in love, but that's what had happened. And now he wanted more. He wanted everything.

So why was he pulled over on the side of the road near

Traub Stables instead of with Maggie, telling her how he felt?

His tires kicked up gravel as he made a quick U-turn and headed toward home.

As he took the stairs two at a time, he could hear Maggie moving around in the spare bedroom. He paused in the doorway to catch his breath and saw she was removing her clothes from the dresser. At first, he actually thought she might be moving her things across the hall to his room.

Then he saw the suitcases open on the bed.

For just a moment, his heart actually stopped beating.

"What are you doing?"

She looked up, and he saw the wet streaks on her cheeks, evidence of the tears she'd recently shed. His heart, beating once again but in a slow, painful rhythm now, twisted inside his chest, because he knew that he was responsible. He'd hurt her and made her cry, and he'd never wanted to do that.

"This is your house," she said to him. "Instead of you always making excuses to run off, I figured it made more sense for me to go."

"Go," he echoed numbly, not wanting to believe it. He'd rushed home to tell her that he loved her—and she was leaving him? He felt as if she'd reached inside his chest and ripped his heart out.

And yet, there was a part of him that wasn't really surprised, that understood he'd been on tenterhooks since their wedding in anticipation of this exact moment. But expecting it didn't mean that he was prepared for it—especially not now. Not when he'd finally accepted how much she meant to him.

"Don't do this," he said. "Please, don't go."

She folded a sweater and placed it in the suitcase. "I can't live like this."

"I know we have some things to figure out, but we can't do that if you're not here."

"I'm not the one who rushed out of here this morning," she pointed out to him.

"I told you where I was going."

"I know," she admitted. "And the fact that you'd rather spend time with a horse than me says everything that needs to be said."

"That's not true," he denied.

"Isn't it?"

"No," he insisted.

But she continued to pack.

"If you won't stay for me, please stay for our baby."

"I'm not going to keep you from our baby," she assured him.

"You don't have to—the twelve hundred miles between here and Los Angeles will do it for you."

"I'm not going back to LA."

"You're not?"

"My job and my life are here now. I have no intention of leaving town. I'm just going to Nina's apartment over the store until I can find something else."

He was torn between relief and confusion. "Why would you stay in Rust Creek Falls if you're not staying with me?"

"I'm staying in Rust Creek Falls because I made a promise to Ben Dalton when he hired me, and I don't renege on my promises."

"Really?" he challenged. "What about the promise you made to me when we exchanged wedding vows?"

She zipped up the first suitcase, and when she looked up at him, the tears that shone in her eyes were like another dagger to his heart. "I would have been happy to love, honor and cherish you for the rest of my life," she said softly, "if I thought there was any chance you might someday feel the same way."

"Wait a minute." He pried her fingers off the handle of her suitcase, linked them with his. "Are you saying that you love me?"

"I would never have married you if I didn't." She kept her gaze riveted on the suitcase as she responded. "But I can't live with someone who doesn't feel the same way."

"But I do," he told her. "I was just too stubborn and stupid to admit—even to myself—how I felt." He nudged her down onto the edge of the mattress, then sat beside her. "I fell for you, hard and fast, even before we were officially introduced. I know it sounds crazy, but it's true. And when you shook my hand—it was like something inside of me just clicked."

She eyed him warily, as if she didn't trust what he was saying. "I thought it was just me."

"And I thought it was just me—until you kissed me."

That first kiss was tame compared to the intimacies they'd shared since then, but her cheeks colored at the memory.

"I think I fell in love with you that night," he told her. "The next morning, I was so happy, certain it was only the first night of many. Then I found out that you were going back to LA that same day.

"And yes, I wondered if our relationship would end the same way my relationship with Shaelyn did. But when you promised to come back, I believed you. I *wanted* to believe you."

"And then I kept making excuses as to why I couldn't," she realized.

He nodded. "And I thought you were brushing me off. I figured you'd gone back to LA and realized you couldn't consider giving up your glamorous life in the city to settle down with a quiet cowboy."

"You barely got a glimpse of my life in LA," she said. "Or you would have known that it wasn't very glamorous."

"But you had palm trees and temperatures that rarely ever dip below freezing."

She managed a small smile. "There is that."

"My point is that I was so worried that you wouldn't want to stay here, with me, that I acted like an idiot in an unsuccessful attempt to protect my heart."

"Are you done acting like an idiot?"

"Probably not completely," he warned. "But I'm done pretending that I don't love you with my whole heart, because I do. And if you can forgive me for being such an idiot, I promise that I will never give you reason to doubt my feelings for you ever again."

"I can forgive you."

He leaned forward and brushed his lips against hers. "I love you, Maggie."

"Show me," she said.

He shoved the suitcases aside, onto the floor, and complied with her request.

Afterward, while their bodies were still joined together and sated from lovemaking, he held her as if he would never let her go. Maggie, her head cushioned on his shoulder, exhaled a soft, contented sigh.

Jesse stroked a hand over her hair, down her back. "I'm sorry."

"For what?"

"Missing out on almost two weeks of mornings just like this because I was an idiot."

"I thought we moved past that part."

"I guess it's easier for you than for me."

She pulled back, just far enough to prop herself up on an elbow so she could see his face. "Well, stop beating up on the man I love."

He lifted a hand to cradle her cheek. "What did I ever do to deserve you?"

"You loved me," she said simply.

"I do," he told her. "You are everything to me—my wife, the mother of my children, my partner in life and the woman I love, for now and forever."

"And you are everything to me," she replied. "My husband, the father of—" Her breath caught as she felt a little flutter low in her belly. "Oh."

His brows lifted. "Oh?"

The flutter happened again, and she took his hand and placed it over the curve of her belly. "Can you feel that?"

"What?" And then he felt it, too. His eyes went wide, his lips curved. "Is that...our baby?"

She nodded. "I think she's happy that her mommy and daddy are finally, truly together."

"And always will be," Jesse promised.

Epilogue

"Thanks for helping me out with this," Nina said to Maggie and Jesse. "The Tree of Hope was a big success last year and I wanted to do it again, but decorating with a baby underfoot turned out to be more difficult than I imagined."

The newlyweds, who had stopped in at Crawford's just to pick up a few staples before Nina conscripted them into service, were happy to help.

"This time next year, we'll have a little one of our own to interfere with our decorating," Maggie said to her husband, already anticipating that day.

Jesse grinned. "An eight-month-old baby whose mother graduated summa cum laude from Stanford Law will probably be directing our every move."

"Unless she takes after her father," his sister teased.

Maggie hooked another ornament over a branch and turned to her sister-in-law. "She?"

"You've slipped up and used the feminine pronoun a few times," Nina told her. "But if the baby's gender is supposed to be a secret, I won't tell."

"I don't know that we'd planned to keep it a secret," Maggie admitted. "But I didn't realize I'd given it away so quickly."

"We only found out at Maggie's ultrasound appointment last week," Jesse told his sister.

Since then—and since his wife's move across the hall

had happily turned "his" bedroom into "their" bedroom—they'd started to set up the nursery in anticipation of their daughter's arrival. Maggie had picked out new paint for the walls and ordered curtains from an online home decor warehouse, and the cradle Jesse had made was already set up in the middle of the room with a big pink bow tied around it.

"Well, I'm thrilled," Nina said. "Because I know Noelle will love having a female cousin to hang out with."

"Does that mean you've given up on the idea of giving her a little sister?"

"No, I still want another baby," Nina confided. "And I think my husband is on board with the plan, but all of the evidence would suggest that Dallas begets boys."

"At least you know Noelle will always have three big brothers to look out for her."

"And I'm sure they'll look out for their little cousin, too," Nina said.

The bell at the front of the store jingled as the door opened and Winona Cobbs entered.

The renowned psychic was a regular customer, usually stopping into the store a couple of times a week to pick up a few things. But this time she chose a cart instead of a basket and moved purposefully through the aisles, filling it with items. Toilet paper, bottled water, canned goods.

"Anticipating a long winter?" Nina asked her.

"There's a storm coming," Winona said.

"Considering it's nearly December in Montana, I'd say you're probably right," Jesse noted drily.

The older woman sent him a dark look as she pushed her cart toward the checkout. "A storm isn't always connected to the weather."

"That was...odd," Maggie said.

"Winona's odd," Nina said, as if that explained everything. "But she wouldn't have the reputation she does if her predictions weren't accurate at least once in a while."

"Even a broken clock can tell time twice a day," Jesse noted.

"You don't believe she has a gift?" Maggie asked him.

"I'm more concerned about finishing this tree so the deserving kids in the community will have gifts," he said, resuming his task.

After the tree was done, Jesse and Maggie headed toward home—just as big fluffy flakes started to fall from the sky, adding to the white blanket that already covered everything in sight.

"It looks like our first Christmas together is definitely going to be a white one," Maggie commented.

"I feel like we've already had Christmas, because I got the greatest gift ever when you became my wife." He gave her a slow, sexy smile that made her knees weak. "And the best part is that you're a gift that can be unwrapped again and again."

She lifted a brow. "Is that a promise?"

"Absolutely," he assured her.

And when they got home, he proved it.

Again and again.

* * * * *

Look for the next installment of the new
Harlequin Special Edition continuity

MONTANA MAVERICKS:
20 YEARS IN THE SADDLE!

Julie Smith never talks about her past—because she has
no memory of anything that happened before she awoke
in a small New England hospital four years ago.
Perhaps a very special cowboy can help bring her
back to her roots...just in time for the holidays!

Don't miss
A VERY MAVERICK CHRISTMAS
by
New York Times *bestselling author Rachel Lee*

On sale December 2014,
wherever Harlequin books are sold.

COMING NEXT MONTH FROM

H HARLEQUIN®

SPECIAL EDITION

Available November 18, 2014

#2371 THE CHRISTMAS RANCH
The Cowboys of Cold Creek • by RaeAnne Thayne

Hope Nichols hadn't found her passion in life...until now. When her relatives decide to shut down the holiday attraction at their Christmas Ranch, Hope leaps into action. She works to make this Christmas the best ever with the help of hunky Rafe Santiago. The former navy SEAL is drawn to the lovely Hope, but a long-buried secret threatens to destroy their burgeoning relationship...

#2372 A BRAVO CHRISTMAS WEDDING
The Bravo Royales • by Christine Rimmer

Aurora Bravo-Calabretti, princess of Montedoro, is used to the best of everything—including men. So when her crush, mountain man Walker McKellan, becomes her bodyguard, Rory is determined to make him hers. There's just one catch—Walker doesn't believe he's right for Rory. Can royal Rory make the Colorado cowboy hers in time for Christmas?

#2373 A ROYAL CHRISTMAS PROPOSAL
Royal Babies • by Leanne Banks

It's Christmastime in Chantaine, and Princess Fredericka Deveraux has returned home with her hearing-disabled son, Leo. When her brother insists that Ericka needs a bodyguard, she disagrees...until she sees her new employee. Former football player Treat Walker is a treat for the eyes—but the princess and her protector both agree they can't act on their mutual attraction. That is, until Santa works his magic under the mistletoe!

#2374 A VERY MAVERICK CHRISTMAS
Montana Mavericks: 20 Years in the Saddle! • by Rachel Lee

Who's that girl? is the question on the lips of everyone in Rust Creek Falls this holiday season. Julie Smith is searching for the answer to that very question. She doesn't know her real name or anything about herself—just that she might discover more in Rust Creek Falls. Local cowboy Braden Traub is drawn to Julie and tries to help her find the key to this puzzle. Can the amnesiac and the maverick solve the mystery of her past in time to create a future together?

#2375 THE LAWMAN'S NOELLE
Men of the West • by Stella Bagwell

Ranch owner Noelle Barnes doesn't need a man—least of all one who's both a handsome member of the wealthy Calhoun clan *and* a lawman. But Evan Calhoun isn't like anyone else she's ever met. For one, he's irresistibly charming. Besides, he wants to use his abilities to do good in their community. As Noelle and Evan's initial disagreements turn into long, sultry nights, the sparks between them might just turn into the fire of love.

#2376 A TEXAS RESCUE CHRISTMAS
Texas Rescue • by Caro Carson

Two outcasts find love as Christmas hits Texas. Former college football player Trey Waterson once suffered a career-ending head injury that impaired some of his cognitive functions. Frustrated, Trey desperately wants to prove himself. His chance comes with heiress Becky Cargill, who's fleeing her malicious mother. When Trey saves Becky's life, sparks fly. But can they move beyond their tragic pasts to find forever together?

YOU CAN FIND MORE INFORMATION ON UPCOMING HARLEQUIN® TITLES, FREE EXCERPTS AND MORE AT WWW.HARLEQUIN.COM.